T0095411

THE MACKENZIE FAMILY

THE MACKENZIE FAMILY

Matheus B. O. E Silva

THE MACKENZIE FAMILY

iUniverse books may be ordered through booksellers or by contacting:

iUniverse
1663 Liberty Drive
Bloomington, IN 47403
www.iuniverse.com
1-800-Authors (1-800-288-4677)

ISBN: 978-1-4917-6531-9 (sc)
ISBN: 978-1-4917-6530-2 (e)

Library of Congress Control Number: 2015905573

Print information available on the last page.

iUniverse rev. date: 5/26/2015

To my aunt, Mariana, and my uncle, Ebert

PROLOGUE

I T WAS A SUNNY AND pleasant afternoon. The wind blew softly, making that day the most relaxing one of the entire summer. But despite the quietness and comfortableness, there was one particular house on Gardenia Street where the residents were having the most unpleasant afternoon.

Adriana sat by the window with a depressed look on her face. Her long red hair was loose, and it covered part of her face. The sunlight that reflected on her brown eyes gave them a grayish appearance. She heard footsteps and turned around to face the newcomer. It was Clark, her boss. He wore a black suit and a gray tie that matched his shirt.

Adriana closed the drapes and came closer to her boss. While she was walking, she adjusted the knot of the apron she was wearing. She and Clark faced each other quietly for a few minutes until he said, "Do you remember the deal?"

"I won't tell, and you won't tell," Adriana said with a mischievous smile.

Clark nodded and walked toward the mansion's entrance. He opened the door and let a man walk in. While the door was still open, Adriana could see two paramedics carrying a body inside an ambulance. The sunlight made all the garden details even more prominent. She could see the fountain spitting water toward the sky, and the lantern path could be seen at a distance. Clark finally closed the door, blocking Adriana's view of the outside.

The two accompanied the man to the living room and sat side by side on the couch. The investigator opted to sit in the chair, facing the residents of the mansion. Adriana withdrew a red scrunchie from her pocket and tied her hair in a long ponytail.

"So," began the detective, "what happened here today?"

"Many things," Adriana replied. "And some more atypical things—"

"Detective Davis, you were aware of my dad's mental issues," Clark said. "But today his outbreaks were even worse. The consequences were—"

Clark covered his face with his hand and started to cry. Adriana put her arm around her boss and faced the detective for a few seconds. The investigator was writing something down in his little black book when Adriana said, "Today Mr. Abromheit had an outbreak before three this afternoon. The attack lasted until the time we made the phone call. It was right before Mrs. Abromheit's death that the boss got his gun and shot himself."

"So your father killed your mother?" Davis asked, writing more things down in his notebook.

"Technically no," Clark replied, sobbing. "When my dad had his outbreak, my mom had a heart attack and couldn't survive it."

"Did she die before or after your father killed himself?"

"After," Adriana said. "When Mr. Abromheit shot himself, his wife went into shock and had the heart attack. It was terrible."

"Well, I believe that I have everything I need," Davis said, closing his black book.

"Thank you for coming, Detective," Clark said, shaking hands with the investigator.

"I was doing my job. I know my way to the door, so don't worry about me."

The detective said good-bye to Adriana and walked away. He closed the door behind him and left. The maid walked toward the window and pushed the drapes aside so she could look outside. The sun was setting. The ambulance was no longer there, and Detective Davis had just entered his car. Clark glanced at his maid for a while and walked away.

"Where are you going?"

"I'm going to my room. I have lots to do."

"Before you go to sleep, don't forget we still have to hide the box," Adriana said, closing the drapes once again.

"Oh—" Clark rolled his eyes. "I forgot about the box. Can we hide it tomorrow?"

"Remember: you have a busy day tomorrow," Adriana replied and smiled. "And why do you want to put off what can be done today?"

"You're probably right," Clark replied.

"Good … I'll get the box, and you can go and organize the room," Adriana said as she entered the kitchen.

Once in the kitchen, Adriana got a shoe box that was on the counter. The maid opened the box and got some stuff out of it. One thing that she took was a folded piece of paper with a big *X* drawn on the back. After she took a quick look, Adriana folded the paper once again and put everything inside the box.

When she got to the second floor, she found Clark standing in front of one of the five rooms in the corridor. She came one step closer to her boss and asked, "Why are we putting the box in your sister's room?"

"Because it's safer and Susan isn't here anymore," Clark answered. "So we've got nothing to worry about."

"But what about your little hobby?" Adriana asked, raising an eyebrow.

"I took care of it."

The maid smiled and walked inside the room. When she got inside, she found several white "bricks" on the bed. She turned to her boss, who was standing just behind her, and asked with certain fear, "Are you going to leave these here?"

"No," Clark explained, "I'm going to store everything inside the cabinet under the sink in the bathroom. Then no one will be able to use this room besides me and you."

"Good, because we don't want you to go to jail," Adriana said. "And what would be the explanation for this room being unusable?"

"Susan's death messed with us, and we're still too traumatized to open the door."

"That could work," Adriana said, walking toward the closet.

She opened the closet door and pushed some clothes off to the left side of it. Adriana gave the shoe box to her boss so she could remove a small hidden panel in the floor of the closet.

Clark gave the box back to his maid so she could put it inside the floor. Adriana covered the secret hole again and organized the clothes. She closed the closet door and stared at her boss for a few seconds until he said, "Now help me to put those bricks in the cabinet under the sink."

"Fine."

They finished the job half an hour later. Adriana went to the kitchen to prepare dinner while Clark waited in his room. Once in the kitchen, the maid filled two pots with water, but while one was half-full, the other one was almost empty.

While she was slicing spices and veggies, Adriana decided to turn on the TV so she could listen to the news of the day. While she was cutting the ingredients, the maid started to think about the recent events that had occurred at the mansion. Once she was done with her thoughts, she put the knife down.

Adriana turned off the TV and got back to her duties. A few moments later, Clark appeared at the kitchen door. He came closer to the maid and said, "I just realized something."

"Me too," Adriana answered while she minced a carrot. "Very interesting, really."

"Really? What did you think about?"

"That you are the sole heir to the family's fortune," the maid replied. "Congratulations, Clark. You are a rich man."

"You want something, don't you?" Clark asked, leaning against the counter.

"Rich and smart! Such a rare combination these days." Adriana smiled deviously. "I don't want much. I just want you to let me live here. And for you to give me a raise—nothing absurd, of course. Let's say 250."

"That's it?"

"Yes," Adriana said and nodded. "But I ask you to keep your mouth shut because if you tell on me—"

"Your request is totally understandable. Consider it included in our deal. You've got nothing to worry about."

"Good. Now what do you want to eat? Chicken or steak?"

"You know what? Let us just order food. I'm gonna spare you tonight."

"You sure?"

"Positively sure," Clark said.

"Great. I'll order sushi, and I'll pay for it," Adriana said, smiling while she turned off the stove.

CHAPTER

1

PRESENT DAY

Samantha Returns

A ROUND EIGHT IN THE MORNING, Erick Woodard, the mailman, arrived at Crystal Street. On that street in particular, people did not pay much attention to their service providers, but Erick Woodard was an exception. Everyone loved him. Maybe it was because of his sympathy, but the mailman had something that caught everyone's attention.

Matt Mackenzie was a seventeen-year-old boy, tall, strong, and very handsome. He lived with his mother, Carla, since his parents had gotten divorced when he was still a baby. Deeper into this family affair, Matt's father left right after he was born and never showed up again. Carlota Mackenzie and her daughter, Cordelia (Carla's mother), helped her to raise her son.

Matt woke at nine on this sunny July morning. He stepped outside in his sleeping shorts to get the newspaper and check the score of the latest Lakers game. Once outside, the boy encountered the mailman, Erick Woodard, kneeling and picking up some envelopes.

"Good morning, Mr. Woodard," Matt said as he kneeled. "Here, let me help you with that."

"Oh, good morning, Matt," the mailman said, smiling his sweet smile. "Thank you."

When they stood up, the mailman got Matt's letters and handed some envelopes to him. The boy thanked Mr. Woodard and stared at him for a couple of seconds. Erick had his sweet look on his face, but he also seemed a little off.

"Mr. Woodard, are you okay? You seem … sad."

"Oh yes. It's my last day. I'm retiring!"

The news came as a bit of shock to Matt. He liked the mailman. Everybody did. And Mr. Woodard didn't seem that old.

"You're seriously retiring?"

"Yup. Since my last heart attack, my doctor told me it was time to back off a little bit," he explained with a sad look on his face.

"Well, we'll sure miss you."

"I'll miss you all as well, especially your family!"

Matt smiled at the mailman and walked away. He entered his house and went to the kitchen to meet his mom, who was making breakfast. He handed her the mail, and she looked at every envelope before she put them in the drawer next to the door.

Carla was a dark-haired woman, not too tall, and extremely beautiful.

"Mr. Woodard is retiring," Matt said, sitting down on the chair next to the table.

"Really?" Carla asked, surprised. "What a shame. I liked that man. So what do you want for breakfast?"

"I'm not hungry."

"Yeah? But you gotta eat."

"Fine. Make me an omelet."

When Carla finished her son's omelet, she started to prepare her own breakfast. When she finally sat down to eat, they heard a scream. Mother and son ran outside their home to see who had screamed.

~oOo~

Ana Mackenzie lived right across the street from her nephew Matt's house. That day she had invited her two sisters, Cordelia and Mery, to join her for breakfast. Ever since they were kids, the bond of the sisters was great, and now as adults, they were even closer.

Cordelia, Matt's grandmother, was the oldest. Every two weeks she'd go to her hairdresser to die the gray hairs that were starting to appear. She was a very beautiful woman, not very tall, and she had piercing green eyes.

Mery and Ana were more alike. They both had brown hair and brown eyes. The only difference between them was Mery's height and age, Ana being the oldest and shortest.

"It's so nice that we do this every week," Cordelia commented as she sipped her coffee.

"Oh yes, but I think we should do it somewhere else," Mery suggested. "We could go to that French bistro … or to the English bakery."

"You know what? That's an excellent idea. I'll do reservations at a nice place for us next week," Ana replied with a smile.

At that moment the doorbell rang, and Ana stood up to answer the door. As she turned the knob and pulled the door open, she was surprised by her mother, Carlota.

Carlota was a woman in her seventies, beautiful and elegant. Her long dark hair was perfectly brushed, and her clothes were perfectly ironed. You could say Carlota was one classy lady.

"Mom, what's up?" Ana asked.

"I needed to talk to you about our lunch today. I'm afraid I'll have to cancel it. Something came up, and I'll have to get it done."

"Oh, don't worry about it. We can have—"

Before Ana could finish her sentence, they heard a scream. The women were quiet for a while until they noticed some unusual movement on the street and decided to check out what had happened.

~oOo~

A group of people was gathered on the street, looking at something. Matt heard someone mention an ambulance. Carla got near so she could see what had happened. She covered her mouth with her hands once she saw the terrible scene. Matt came closer to his mother and his eyes widened once he saw what everybody was staring at. Erick Woodard was laying on the ground, covered in letters and bills.

When the paramedics arrived a few minutes later, they gave the news everybody was dreading. Erick Woodard had suffered a massive heart attack that had killed him right on the spot.

Hours later the residents of Crystal Street gathered at Carlota Mackenzie's house, Matt's great-grandmother, to work on the details for the deceased mailman's funeral. Carlota served some snacks with soft drinks, tea, and juice.

Helena Trevers said she would be in charge of the flowers, while Ana Mackenzie would set the date at the church. Every single neighbor decided to say something so they could give Erick Woodard a dignified good-bye.

When the residents went back to their places, the Mackenzies were the only ones left. They gathered at Carlota's living room and were all so shocked with the recent events.

"It's ironic," Cordelia said. "Most people die before, during, or right after their retirement."

"I retired ten years ago and I'm still alive," Carlota replied.

"That's why I used the word *most*," Cordelia answered with a smile.

"I still can't believe this happened," Carla commented. "Erick was such a good person."

"That's why we say that the good ones are the first to die," Ana answered, glancing at her mother.

"I don't why, but I have the feeling you're trying to tell me something," Carlota said.

"If you wanna take that bullet—" Ana replied and laughed, which gave the others a few laughs afterward.

"Well," Matt said, "I'm going home."

~oOo~

The mailman's funeral happened on Wednesday of that week. The whole neighborhood was there. After the service, everyone followed the priest to the cemetery where Erick Woodard was going to be buried. At the end of the burial, a few people joined the Mackenzies at Helena Trevers's house for a brunch that Mery Mackenzie had prepared.

Everyone paid a beautiful homage to the mailman. It sounds extreme when a whole neighborhood gets together to do a thing like that, but Erick Woodard was special. Beside his sympathy and goodwill, the mailman had something else in him. Problem was that nobody ever knew what it was.

On the Thursday following the burial, people had yet to accept Erick's death, but as life went on, everybody returned to their normal lives with the intention of forgetting that devastating tragedy.

That afternoon a moving truck arrived. As usual, the Mackenzie family members gathered at Carlota's front yard, which was the best view on the street, so they could snoop around the new neighbors.

As the movers moved the furniture from the truck to the house, the new neighbors did not show up. It wasn't until a few minutes later when a silver Mercedes stopped right in front of Carlota's house. When the engine was turned off, the car doors were opened, and a couple got out of the vehicle.

The woman was tall and thin with blonde hair and beautiful blue eyes. Her husband was tall, strong, and very charming. The couple approached the neighbors who stared at them with their mouths opened. The woman smiled and removed her glasses.

"You can close your mouths, as you are not fish," she said.

"Oh my gosh," Mery said. "Who knew the wind would blow you this way again."

"So you're back?" Ana asked.

"Yes, and this time with a husband!" the beauty replied, pulling her husband by the arm. "Honey, this is everybody. Everybody, this is Gregory."

"Everybody? I feel nameless." Cordelia laughed, shaking hands with Gregory. "Hello, I'm Cordelia. Nice to meet you. And it's good to see you again, Samantha."

"You know each other?" Matt's cousin, Thales, asked.

"Yes," Samantha said and giggled. "I used to live here."

"She moved away a couple of months before you were born," Carlota explained. "And now she's returned after eighteen years."

Carlota decided to invite everyone inside for a cup of tea. She served a hot drink accompanied by some cookies that she had baked the day before. Samantha and Gregory sat in the corner and shared one cup of tea. Carla and Matt sat next to Carlota on the couch while the others spread through the living room.

"So, Samantha, what made you come back?" Ana asked with certain curiosity.

"Well, I left to go look for a man. Someone nice and caring who shared my interests. That's when I met Gregory and fell in love. When we got married, I saw that there was no other reason to stay away," Samantha explained.

"And for how long have you been married?" Thales asked.

"That's where our story gets interesting." The woman giggled again. "It took me a few years to persuade him to get married. Five years to be exact. So we dated for three years, and it took me five to persuade him. We've been married for ten years."

"And do you work, Gregory?" Mery asked while she dipped a cookie in her tea.

"Yes," the man answered, "I am a prosecutor."

"Nice!" Matt replied.

"A very good one if you'd like to know," Samantha answered instead of her husband. "He put a lot of people in jail. People who deserved it, of course."

"Ah … so your life must be pretty exciting!" Mery said.

"I wouldn't say that," Gregory replied. "But I assure you it's not boring."

~oOo~

After the reunion at Carlota's house, Samantha and her husband went back to their new home. When they got there, the movers had already organized the furniture the way Samantha recommended before the moving happened.

The couple went to their room on the second floor. The suite was huge, with an enormous bathroom and a closet that would make anyone jealous. Gregory removed his leather coat and hung it on the hanger next to the chiffonier. Samantha sat on the bed and removed her shoes and earrings.

"I liked the new neighbors," Gregory said, taking his pants off.

"They're great!" Samantha replied. "But lying to them, my friends, is something that's really hard for me."

"You don't seem exactly happy to move back here …" Gregory said as he walked toward his wife.

"No, believe me … I am happy," the woman answered. "It's just … I don't wanna lie to them, not while we had so much fun together."

"I know. But you know that lying is needed. No one can know what happened here," Gregory said before he kissed his wife's forehead.

"No one will know," Samantha concluded. "But promise me one thing. If he comes back, you're gonna kill him."

"I promise."

~oOo~

The next day Samantha walked out of her house and stopped at every house on Crystal Street, distributing invitations for a barbecue she was going to throw for the neighbors on Sunday. Of course, everyone RSVP'd. After all, no one had seen Samantha Roberts in eighteen years.

When the guests started to arrive at Samantha's house on Sunday, they marveled at the backyard. The place looked like a small forest, and the pool looked like a lake among the vegetation. This scene was enough to invite questions about money.

"How much money does he make per year?" an old lady asked.

"He must be more successful than we think!" another one commented.

"How many people does he steal from to have all this kind of money?"

As you may well see, there were all sorts of questions, and some of them were pretty rude and offensive, if not all of them.

Besides the number of people gathered in her backyard, Samantha's attention was stuck with her best friends, all of them members of the Mackenzie family.

"You're just saying that to flatter us," Mery said, laughing.

"No!" Samantha said and giggled. "I'm serious. I missed you a lot these past eighteen years. Your joy and unity is contagious! It's not easy to let that go."

"Samantha, I wanna change the subject a little bit here," Carlota said. "But your house is absolutely beautiful! I don't recall any houses that beautiful here on Crystal Street."

"Thank you."

"But that wasn't your house, am I right?" Carla asked. "You lived at—"

"Helena's!" Ana said. "I remember that when Samantha left, Ana moved in."

"You're right," Cordelia said. "Helena's been living here for so long I usually forget that she moved in after you left."

Samantha took a sip of her wine and waited a few minutes to ask a question that was on her mind since the day she had arrived.

"When I moved back, I noticed that a lot of people were acting strange. I got this weird vibe."

"Oh yes," Matt said. "Do you remember Erick Woodard?"

"Sure!" Samantha said with enthusiasm. "Erick Woodard, the best mailman ever!"

"Well, he passed away last week," the boy answered.

"What? No way!"

"It's true … unfortunately," Thales said. "The whole street prepared the funeral. It was really beautiful."

"Well, you must take me to the cemetery," Samantha said, pointing at Mery. "I gotta give Erick a proper good-bye!"

In the end, Samantha's barbecue was a success. People loved the food, the company, and mostly the return of a great old friend. Just like her neighbors, Samantha was also very happy. After all, she had come back home, a place she loved and always regretted leaving behind.

CHAPTER

2

The Man of the Coffee Place

S HE SERVED HER GUEST AND only then poured the tea in her own cup. Carla put three biscuits on Samantha's plate, and she thanked her with a brief nod. A few minutes later Matt came down the stairs and greeted the women.

"Where are you going?" Carla asked her son as he passed by the kitchen door.

"I'm going to meet some friends at the coffee shop," the boy replied.

"Drive safe."

The boy nodded and left the house. When he closed the door, Samantha sighed oddly. Carla noticed her friend's strange behavior and asked, "What's wrong?"

"Oh, nothing." Samantha smiled, though she was a little saddened.

"Samantha, we've known each other for almost thirty years. I think I know when you're lying or not."

"I'm going through a bad time lately. I got pregnant two years ago."

"And you lost the baby?" Carla asked.

Samantha nodded with tears in her eyes. Carla sighed and touched her friend's shoulder as an act of kindness. There wasn't much to be done in those situations.

"You know, you could always try again," Carla said.

"We have been trying. But nothing happened until now, and Greg really wants a baby."

"Are you worried?"

"Very!" Samantha asked, touching her forehead. "I'm scared that if I don't give him a baby he might leave me."

"What?" Carla asked, perplexed. "Honey, no! No, no, no. Gregory's not gonna leave you. He's crazy about you!"

"Do you really think so?" Samantha asked, drying her tears.

"I'm sure," Carla replied, smiling. "Give it some time. In the end, everything will turn out just fine."

~oOo~

When Gregory Desmond came back home, Samantha was in the kitchen making dinner. He walked in and gave his wife a kiss. She smiled and threw some carrots in a pot.

"What are we having tonight?" he asked.

"Stew," Samantha answered. "I know how much you like it."

"And how was your day?" Greg asked while he was getting a can of Coke out of the fridge.

"It was good. I spent the afternoon at Carla's. We had tea and talked for a bit," Samantha explained.

"Oh … and what did you talk about?" he asked.

"Nothing much," Samantha replied. "But I did have to tell her a little white lie."

"Another one?" Gregory asked.

"What do you want me to do?" Samantha asked as she threw the knife on the counter. "I'm sad, and my friends know me well enough to realize I'm not okay! I cannot tell the truth, so I gotta keep making up lies!"

"And that's all because of something you did!" Gregory yelled in reply as he threw his soda can on the floor.

"Oh, so now this is my fault?" Samantha laughed in complete perplexity. "I made a mistake? Yes, but you could've avoided this web of lies if you had killed Jack Stappord when you had the chance!"

~oOo~

The next day Carla called her aunts Mery and Ana so they could talk about her recent conversation with Samantha. While they talked in the kitchen, Thales and Matt decided to join the ladies.

"So Samantha lost a baby?" Ana asked while she tasted her coffee.

"Yes," Carla answered, "and she's afraid that Gregory is gonna leave her."

"Well, if he does that, he's a complete idiot," Mery said. "He's gonna dump her just because she can't give him a child? That's not a motive."

"Can't he adopt?" Matt asked. "I agree with Aunt Mery. If Gregory knows Samantha can't have kids, why won't he adopt?"

"Because most of the time people don't feel comfortable raising another person's baby," Ana explained. "I know what she's going through."

"No, you don't," Thales said. "Am I adopted?"

"No," Ana said and laughed. "But I thought about adopting. But the year after that thought, you were born."

Thales hugged his mother and left the kitchen. Matt kissed his mother and left as well. The girls kept chatting, but a few moments later Carla stood up and said, "Well, girls, I gotta go. I'm meeting Samantha at the coffee place."

"Oh—" Mery said in excitement. "I hope you come back with more gossip."

~oOo~

Someone knocked on the office door. The gray-haired man who sat behind a glass table faced the door and pressed a button to unlock it.

The door opened, and another man walked in the office. He was tall, extremely thin, and ugly as hell. His crooked and rotten teeth contributed to the terrible bad breath that was a perfect match for his greasy hair, which was filled with dandruff.

"Hello, Jack," the man said, smiling.

Jack, the gray-haired businessman, swallowed vomit after he smelled his colleague's dreadful breath and said, "Bill, you've got news for me?"

"Yeah," Bill answered, "I found them. They moved. They're now living in a suburb, some street named Crystal."

"Oh … so she came home," Jack said and then laughed. "Great—"

"What should I do?" the putrid man asked.

"What you do best," Jack replied. "But you will need a gun—"

~oOo~

The next morning the members of the Mackenzie family gathered at Carlota's house for breakfast. The matriarch served a great variety of fruits, juices, breads, and cheeses, so her relatives could taste everything.

While they were eating, the family chatted and laughed at the jokes they told one another. Once they were done, the women went to the kitchen with Carlota to help clean up the mess while Thales and Matt went to the living room.

A few minutes later the rest of the family joined the boys, who were talking about a new game that was about to be released. Moments later the doorbell rang. Carlota stood up and answered the door.

"Diane?" the Mackenzie matriarch asked when she saw the visitor. "What are you doing here?"

Diane Thompson was the mayor's wife. David Thompson was a great friend of Carlota's late husband. Of course, Diane and Carlota were always best friends, but after her husband's election Diane moved away from suburbia and started to live in Greendale's downtown.

"Hello, Carlota," Diane replied. "Long time no see."

"Indeed. Can I help you with something?"

"As you might as well know," Diane said, "I throw a party at my house every year, and I would love for you to come. You can bring someone if you want."

Diane handed a beautiful envelope to her friend, and Carlota picked it up with certain surprise. Carlota analyzed the invitation but didn't say a word until Diane asked, "Did something happen?"

"Umm … not exactly. But when my husband was alive, we used to be best friends," Carlota answered. "But when your husband got elected, you turned your back on me."

"Carlota, don't be ridiculous," Diane said and giggled, a bit embarrassed.

"I am not being ridiculous!" the Mackenzie matriarch replied. "I am being honest! I've seen your parties in the newspapers throughout the years, and I don't recall being invited to any of them!"

Diane Thompson was quiet for a few minutes. Carlota stared at her *friend* but did not say a word. The Mackenzie matriarch sighed and pushed the door in an attempt to close it, but Diane stopped her from doing so.

"Don't do this … please."

"What do you want?" Carlota asked, irritated. "Like it wasn't enough turning your back on someone who once considered you a sister. Now you come here and invite me to a fucking party like nothing ever happened?"

"I am so sorry," Diane said. "I've been so unhappy these past years! David is never around. His career is at the peak!"

"So you thought that you could rely on a friend?" Carlota asked, smiling.

"Exactly," Diane replied.

"Well, you thought wrong!" Carlota yelled. "Why don't you go back to your manor and call one of those bitches you've been in the newspapers with? They seem to be the only *friends* you've got left!"

Carlota slammed the door and returned to the living room. Her relatives were all staring at her, bewildered by her rudeness, but she pretended not to notice. Matt slid his chair a little bit and made room for his great-grandmother to sit down. She put the invitation to Diane's party in the center of the table and said, "What do you think I should do?"

"Honestly?" Ana asked. "I think you should go to this party."

"Diane might've been wrong," Cordelia agreed, "but you were the one who taught us not to hold on to rage."

"Fine!" Carlota said at last. "I'm going to this bloody party, but I'm taking one of you with me."

~oOo~

Around three in the afternoon of the following day, Mery heard her doorbell ring. She ran to the door and received Samantha with open arms. The neighbor walked into her friend's house and followed her to the kitchen. Mery washed her hands and went back behind the counter.

"Do you mind if we talk in here?"

"Not at all!" Samantha replied.

"Thanks! I need to finish this cake," Mery said. "It's Helena's birthday tonight."

"Oh yes," Samantha said, putting her purse on a chair next to her. "She invited me, but I don't know if I'll be able to attend. Gregory and I have an event downtown. He's in line for a promotion."

"Oh my God! That's great!" Mery said, waving her hands. "I'm sure Helena will understand. But changing the subject, what can I do for you?"

"Yes!" Samantha yelled with enthusiasm.

She grabbed her purse and picked out a folded piece of paper. After she unfolded the paper, she handed it to Mery, who read the document carefully. Samantha stared at her friend for a few seconds and asked, "So what do you think?"

"You're organizing a charity event?" Mery asked.

"Yes," Samantha answered. "I've always done charity, at least during the years I lived here. After more than ten years without doing anything like it, I believe it's time for me to get back to my activities."

"Well, that is great! If you need any help, count me in!"

"I'm not sure yet about what I'll do to raise money, but I'll think of something."

~oOo~

Matt closed the car door and walked around the vehicle to help a girl step out. She was more or less his age, probably one year younger. She had golden hair and green eyes like emeralds.

Both walked toward the mall's entrance, and once inside, they headed to Macy's. The girl wanted to buy a dress for Helena's birthday later that day.

"What do you think about this dress?" Sarah asked. "I think it looks like an old lady's dress."

"It does," Matt said and giggled. "But you can take that one."

The boy pointed at the dress that the mannequin was wearing. The dress was blue with a low neckline and a skirt that ended just above the knee. Sarah examined the dress for a little bit and smiled.

Matt called for the salesgirl and asked for a dress that would fit Sarah. A few minutes later, the girl came back with two pieces of clothing. They were identical except for the color variation.

"We have these two kinds—red and blue," the salesgirl said.

"Ah, thank you!" Sarah said. She got the dresses and entered the fitting room.

Matt followed the girl and sat on a chair outside the fitting room. A few moments later Matt heard Sarah's voice coming from inside the fitting room.

"Matt? Could you help me with the zipper?"

"Umm … sure," he replied.

Matt stood up and walked toward fitting room number three, where his date was. He knocked three times, and when Sarah opened the door, he was mortified. The girl was only wearing her silk white bra and nothing more.

"Sarah," he said.

"Don't just stand there. People might see!"

She grabbed Matt by the shirt and pulled him inside the fitting room and then locked the door immediately.

~oOo~

Carla was in the kitchen baking a lemon pie, a dessert she would bring to Helena's party. She got half a lemon and squeezed it on a creamy mixture that was in the mixer. Suddenly her phone rang. Carla reached down and picked up the extension that was on the wall next to the door.

"Hello? Yes, this is she. *He did what?*"

~oOo~

Matt and Sarah were at the security office at the mall when Carla walked in, completely irritated. Sarah's mother followed. Matt and Sarah stared at their respective mothers, both of whom were furious. The security guard accompanied the women to another room so they could talk.

"Don't worry, officer. This will never happen again," Sheila said.

"Yes," Carla agreed, "we're gonna talk to our kids and work this mess out."

"I hope you do, ma'am," the officer said. "You know they could've been arrested, right?"

"Of course!" Sheila said. "But you can relax. What happened here today will never happen again."

The women left the room and nodded so their kids would follow them outside. When they reached the parking lot, Carla turned around and said, "I can't believe you did that!"

"We're sorry. This wasn't supposed to happen," Sarah said.

"Me and Carla hope that this doesn't happen again!" Sheila replied. "You know what consequences this little *escapade* of yours could've brought?"

"Yes," Matt answered, "we promise this will never happen again."

"What I cannot understand is why in the mall—" Carla said. "You two have been together for months now."

"Carla's right," Sheila said and nodded. "You two are together for months. If you want to have sex, you could do it in our house or at Matt's house or inside the car in one of the garages."

"Mom!" Sarah said, embarrassed. "We know. We won't do it outside anymore."

"Great!" Carla concluded. "Now let's go home. I still have to finish Helena's pie."

"Lemon?" Sheila asked.

"Yup."

"See ya in a couple of hours."

~oOo~

At eight o'clock the guests started to arrive. Helena was at the door, greeting everyone with great enthusiasm. Her shiny green dress gave her a younger appearance, and so did her hair, which was pulled back in a long ponytail she had her hairdresser make for her, probably with the help of extensions.

Helena was known for her perfection addiction. In the backyard, the tables were spread out, one next to the other, with the same amount of chairs around each of them. The plates and silverware and glasses were counted out by the same number of people who RSVP'd. Inside the house, Helena had stored a few more glasses and plates in case someone broke one. The music was at the right volume not to disturb anyone. Short version? Everything was perfect.

"Thank you for coming, Carlota," Helena said when the Mackenzie matriarch arrived. "You and your family are very important to me."

"Oh, thank you!" Carlota said and smiled. "Here's your gift! I hope you like it."

"Thanks!"

Carlota went to the backyard, where her family was gathered and chatting about something. Carlota greeted everyone, and they greeted her back as she sat next to Matt.

"So what are you talking about?" she asked.

"Matt fucked at the mall today!" Ana said.

"You did what?"

"Long story," Matt answered. "Yes, I had sex at the mall, but which one of you never did it?"

"I never fucked at the mall," Mery said.

"I fucked at the bar once," Ana replied, laughing.

"What?" Thales asked in shock. "I'm not listening to this."

Everyone started to laugh when the boy left the table. Cordelia stared at the house for a moment and saw Samantha coming out to the backyard.

"Samantha's here!" she said.

"Really?" Mery asked. "She told me she wasn't coming. She and Gregory had an event today."

"Oh yeah," Ana replied to her sister. "She told me about that earlier. Gregory went alone."

In this moment Matt got his phone out of his pocket and read something on the screen. He stood up and put his phone away once again.

"Sarah's here. Excuse me."

When the boy walked away, Carla turned to her mother and said, "See? He only cares about the girlfriend now."

"Oh, honey," Cordelia said. "That's common. I know they've been together for a few months now, but you gotta get used to it. It will take time, yes, but it will go away. Besides, she's a nice girl, and you know it."

"Yeah," Carla replied, "and if he's happy—"

"Stop your whining!" Carlota said all of a sudden. "You stop thinking about his relationship and get one all to yourself. It's been twelve years since his father left. It's time for you to go back in the game!"

Carlota spanked her butt and giggled.

"You know," Carla said, "for a seventy-year-old woman you have a very fertile imagination."

"Not just my mind, dear," Carlota said and laughed. "But for a seventy-year-old woman I've got a more active sex life than you do."

"Now I cannot hear this," Ana said, standing up and laughing.

Samantha approached Mery and greeted her. Both decided to go and chat inside the house to get away from all the noise. They sat on the couch and started to talk about the fund-raising event Samantha was planning.

"So did you think about the event?" Mery asked.

"Yes!" Samantha answered in excitement. "I'm gonna throw a talent show."

"Talent show?"

"Precisely," the blonde replied. "Everything will take place here at Crystal Street. The people who want to perform can sign in with you, and the rest can buy tickets with me."

"That sounds good," Mery commented. "Are you performing?"

"I might do a dancing act, but nothing's confirmed," Samantha explained. "But the winner is getting a trophy or medal. I didn't think about that just yet."

The women kept chatting when they were suddenly surprised by someone they'd never expected to see at Helena's party. Mery stood up and greeted the new arrival.

"Diane, this is a surprise. How did you know we'd be here?"

"I went to Carlota's house, and one of your neighbors told me that I could find her here," Diane explained. "Can I talk to her?"

"Sure. Let me get her for you," Mery answered.

"There will be no need for that, Mery," Carlota said, walking into the living room. "Samantha, do you think you and Mery could give us some privacy?"

"Certainly," Samantha and Mery answered in unison.

Mery was the first to leave the room. Samantha followed her and crossed paths with Diane. The moment the two crossed, they heard glass breaking. Carlota turned around to see what had happened, and that was when she saw the little hole in the window. Suddenly Diane Thompson fell on the floor.

"Diane?" Carlota called.

The first lady of Greendale did not move. Samantha stared at the woman and started to scream when she saw blood spreading on the floor. Mery covered her mouth with her hands, in a state of complete shock. It was a matter of seconds until all the guests at Helena's party gathered in the living room.

"Someone call an ambulance!" Carlota shouted as she kneeled near her friend. "Oh my God—"

Matt got his phone out of his pocket and dialed 911. Sarah held her boyfriend's arm, and he took her out of the room. Carla followed her son and his girlfriend while Cordelia ran toward her mother, who cried over her friend's body.

~oOo~

Needless to say, after the incident, Helena's party came to an end. While Carla, Cordelia, Ana, and Mery joined Carlota at the hospital, the other guests went back to their homes with one question in mind. Who could've shot Diane Thompson?

"Why would someone shoot her?" Thales asked.

Matt was sitting in front of his computer while his cousin walked around the bedroom. Sarah was lying on the bed, playing something on her phone. Matt stood up and answered his cousin's question.

"She's the mayor's wife. People have reasons to shoot her."

"No," Thales said, "people have reasons to shoot David, but not her."

"Have you ever wondered—" Sarah said, putting her phone down, "that a lot of people have reasons to want David dead? Why not make him vulnerable first?"

"Like I said," Matt replied, "people have reasons to want Diane dead. Question is, how did they know she was here?"

"Someone must've followed her," Sarah answered. "These people—shooters, killers, or whatever—are usually hired by someone. Those politicians would not put dirt on their own hands."

"Okay," Thales said, "but who could've followed her here?"

"I don't know," Matt answered. "But you know what? This ain't our business, so we'd better butt out."

~oOo~

Carlota walked into the waiting room with swollen and red eyes, probably because of the crying. Cordelia hugged her mother and helped her to sit down on the couch. Carla, Mery, and Ana came closer and asked for news regarding Diane.

"I spoke with the doctor," Carlota said. "She's gonna be okay. The bullet didn't hit any organs, and they've already finished surgery. Diane's asleep."

"Thank God," Ana said, touching her chest.

"Did you call David?" Carla asked.

"I called him," Mery answered. "He told me he'd be here as soon as possible."

The waiting room doors opened, and David Thompson came in running. The mayor was in his sixties. He wore a gray suit and a black tie over a white shirt. He looked nervous and worried, and once he saw Carlota, he ran toward her.

"Oh, David!" she said, standing up and hugging her friend.

"What happened?" he asked with tears in his eyes.

"She got shot," Carlota explained. "We don't know who did it, but she'll be okay. The doctor has finished surgery, and Diane's sleeping now."

"Thank God," he said, sighing. "And thanks for calling me."

"We had to," Mery said. "You're her husband. But I suggest you hire a few bodyguards from now on. And order a police investigation."

"I will," David answered. "Now, if you'll excuse me, I have to go and see my wife."

"I'll take you there," Carlota said, standing up.

~oOo~

Carla and Helena sat in Le Petit Café's outdoor seating, chatting over their drinks. She then tasted the juice and cleared her throat. Helena, who sat right in front of her, waited until she was ready to start a conversation. The women were quiet for a few moments, and then Carla said, "I am so sorry for the way your party ended."

"Oh, don't be," Helena answered. "It was unfortunate, yes, but we couldn't have predicted it."

"Yes … sadly."

"How's Carlota doing?" Helena asked, sipping her coffee.

"She's pretty shaken up about it," Carla replied. "She and Diane were friends for years. Although they were estranged for a time, a true friendship is never actually over."

"That's true, a real friendship never ends," Helena said.

Carla smiled. "Helena, could you wait for a moment? Matt asked me to buy breakfast for him and Sarah."

"She slept at your place?"

"Yes, she called her mother and told Sheila what happened and said she wanted to stay with Matt. Sheila said yes, and I'm not gonna kick the girl out of my house," Carla explained.

"But don't you ever get worried? That she might … you know?" Helena asked.

"Of course I do! What mother wouldn't? Sheila has the same preoccupation, but we talked to them after the mall incident, so—"

Helena smiled but said nothing. Carla still sensed her disapproval. Carla stood up and went inside the coffee shop. She got some cheese and bread, a couple of jelly pots, and cream cheese and took everything to the checkout booth.

While she was waiting in the line, Carla looked outside observing the movement of the clientele. The place was really famous. At all times, Le Petit Café had people coming in and out. It was finally her turn.

Carla put her things on the counter, and suddenly a man appeared right in front of her and started to chat with the checkout girl. Carla stared at him in complete perplexity and poked him on the shoulder.

"Excuse me, sir. I don't know if you noticed, but there's a line for you to wait your turn."

"Oh—" the man said, turning around to face Carla.

He was tall and strong, and he had deep eyes. He had a deep voice that perfectly matched with his gray hair, which further increased his charm. Carla's eyes sparkled for a bit, but she soon forgot about the Greek god standing in front of her and said, "*Oh?* That's the only word you know?"

"No, I'm sorry," he answered. "I was in the line, but I had to go back there and get a bottle of milk."

"So you should go back to the end of the line," Carla replied.

"Fine," the man answered. "I'm so sorry."

Carla nodded, and the man walked away. She looked back, but she couldn't find the guy, so she kept looking until she heard the checkout girl calling for her. Carla smiled idiotically and paid for her stuff. Once she sat down again at her table, Helena smiled and said, "Who was that man?"

"I don't know. Just some jerk who was trying to cut the line," Carla answered.

"And did you let him cut it?" Helena asked.

"Um … no!"

"Carla! C'mon! Did you see his butt? Oh my gosh! It was perfect! And you've been single for far too long. And hear me out—he was into you."

"What?" Carla asked. "No, he wasn't!"

"Yes, he was!" Helena replied. "And you were into him as well."

"Okay, now you're just being ridiculous."

"Really?" Helena asked ironically. "Then tell me what you were looking for when he walked way."

"I was looking for—" Carla said. "Oh, fine! I was looking for him."

"I knew it!" Helena shouted and applauded, making sure everyone stared at her.

CHAPTER

3

A Date

MATT AND SARAH TURNED INTO an aisle to look for a movie. After they searched for several minutes, the boy found what he was looking for. He brought the movie to his mother, who stood on the other side of the store. Carla took the object and glanced at her son.

"No," she said, "I'm not giving you money to buy this."

"But, Mom!" Matt protested. "It's just a movie."

"We're not here to buy a movie," Carla replied. "We're here to buy Sheila a birthday present! So Sarah, please tell me what your mother would like from this store."

"She likes to cook, and she kept talking about a new cookbook that was just released," Sarah answered. "So I guess she'd probably like that."

"Awesome!" Carla said.

Matt stared at his girlfriend, and she giggled. The boy put the movie on top of some books and walked away with the girl. Carla started to look for the cookbook when someone poked her shoulder. When she turned around, she widened her eyes.

"Excuse me," the man said. "I'm trying to look at this shelf, but you're blocking me."

"Ah," Carla replied, rolling her eyes. "You're the guy from the coffee shop. Well, since you tried cutting in the line that day, I'm sure you won't mind me staying in front of you."

"Actually I will mind," he answered. "But you can stay right next to me if you want. That way we could both take a look at the shelf."

"Umm—" Carla sighed. "I'd rather not."

She turned around and walked away, but she stopped walking when she heard her *friend* say, "I love this movie!"

When Carla turned around, the man was holding up the movie Matt had showed her before. She approached the man and grabbed the movie.

"My son gave this to me. I almost forgot! Thanks," she said and walked away.

After Carla found the cookbook, she paid for it along with Matt's movie. When they left the store, they headed to the mall parking lot. Matt and Sarah sat on a bench while Carla paid the valet.

"Hello again."

Carla turned around and faced the same man from the coffee shop. She rolled her eyes and said, "Jeez … are you following me?"

"No, you're the one who seems to frequent the same places I do."

"Well, have a great day."

"You know," he said, "we met yesterday, and we ran into each other twice today. I don't think this was a mere coincidence. What do you say about having dinner with me?"

"Tonight?" Carla asked.

"Yes."

"I can't tonight. Or tomorrow," she answered. "But I might be free on Friday."

"Right," he said and handed her a card. "Here's my card. Call me when you're available."

"I certainly will … Clark."

~oOo~

Mery came out of the kitchen carrying a tray that held a carafe of lemonade and some snacks for her guest and friend, Samantha. The blonde beauty sat by the head of the table and carried a big heavy file. Mery put the tray on the table and sat down.

Samantha put the file on the table and opened it. She pulled out a huge amount of paper from inside and threw the file on an empty chair and said, "Well, here are the charity events I've already done. There's the masquerade ball, the fashion show—anyway, all of them."

"So you've really decided on the talent show?" Mery asked.

"Yes, but we still need to work on a few kinks," Samantha answered. "I have already sent the flyers to the graphics place so they could be printed. We will distribute them in the neighborhood. Now let's talk about decorations."

"About that," Mery said. "I don't think we should spend money on this. Let people spend their own money on the material they'll need for their performances."

"Your thought is almost like mine," Samantha said. "We shall only spend money with the lighting and sound system. That's what will be needed for the event."

"I totally agree," Mery answered.

"Awesome! Now let's talk about ticket prices," Samantha replied.

"Right. I was thinking fifteen to twenty dollars."

"Twenty-five," Samantha concluded. "Well, I guess we're all set!"

"If you say so—" Mery replied, a bit annoyed.

~oOo~

The nurse came into Diane Thompson's room and found the mayor sleeping on the chair. His legs were straight. Half his butt was out of the seat, and his head was completely skewed. The woman poked the man on the chest, and he jumped.

"What happened?"

"Nothing," the nurse answered. "But I think you should go home and sleep properly."

"I cannot leave her," the mayor said.

"She won't be alone," the woman said and smiled. "I'm here, and she has a friend outside."

When David left the room, he met Carlota sitting in the corridor. She stood up and hugged her friend. Carlota put her hand on his shoulder and massaged it for a bit.

"Let's go to the cafeteria," she said. "You need something."

Once in the cafeteria, Carlota went to the counter and ordered two grilled cheeses and two cups of coffee and cream. Minutes later the waitress brought the order to the table, and David started to eat. It seemed like he hadn't eaten for days. When he finished eating, Carlota said, "David—"

"No," he answered, "I'll be doing the talking here. Carlota, I am so thankful to have you as a friend. What you did for Diane these past few days, staying here, taking care of her—"

"You don't have to thank me," Carlota replied. "Diane is my friend. What else could I have done?"

"You could've done nothing!" David said. "And that's what I like about you. You're an amazing woman. Your husband and I were great friends once. But when I got into politics, we grew apart. I was devastated when I learned of his death, but I did not reach out to you. I was too busy with my career."

"David, you don't need to explain yourself," Carlota said, combing her hair with her fingers. "My husband died many years ago. My daughters were still kids. I know we were estranged for several years, but the care I feel for you continues till today. I was furious when Diane rang my doorbell and invited me to her party. Now I realize that was an honest apology. Well, I'm headed to her room. You go home and rest and keep my sandwich."

"Oh—" David answered with a smile. "Thank you!"

~oOo~

Mery and Ana sat on the front porch of Helena's house, drinking beer. The owner of the house came outside a few moments later, carrying a bucket with ice and a few more bottles of the drink. The three ladies talked about the recent conversation Mery had with Samantha. While Mery babbled about everything, Ana and Helena just listened, drank, and waited to express their thoughts.

"So I don't know why she needs me," Mery said. "She vetoed all my ideas, except when I said there was no need for decorations. But if she can decide everything by herself, why ask me for help?"

"Well, we all know Samantha likes to be the center of attention," Ana replied as she shook her bottle of beer. "She's a good friend, but she likes to steal the spotlight."

"Yeah," Helena agreed, "I've organized several events with this lady I knew before I moved here, and she did exactly the same."

"Well, maybe the right thing to do is tell her how you feel," Ana said as she sipped her beer.

"How?" Mery asked. "*Stop pissing me off, you bleached bitch?* No, I like Sam. She's just a very complicated person to deal with."

"Then why did you call us here to bitch about her?" Helena asked.

"Because I need an excuse to drink!" Mery laughed, which made the other girls laugh as hard as she did.

~oOo~

Thales and Matt were in the room playing a video game when Ana knocked on the door and came into her son's bedroom. She kissed them on the forehead and left. They kept playing until Matt's phone vibrated. He read the message on the screen and said, "I have to go."

"Already?" Thales asked.

"Yes, today is Sarah's mother's birthday. Mom and I are going to their house in a bit, but I gotta get ready."

"Fine."

Matt grabbed his stuff that lay on his cousin's bed and walked toward the door, but Thales called to him. Matt turned around and faced his cousin.

"What?"

"I have to talk to you," Thales said.

"Can't it wait till after the party?" Matt asked, checking his watch.

"Sure."

"Awesome!"

~oOo~

The next day the flyers Samantha ordered for her talent show were delivered to her house. The minute they arrived she called Mery so they could distribute them throughout Crystal Street. They stapled the flyers on poles and left some on the mailboxes. It was only a matter of time till the neighbors saw the advertisement and started to share the information with their friends.

On that same afternoon Samantha got several phone calls regarding the event. She sent them all to Mery since she was responsible for the tickets and registrations.

It was a really busy day, especially for those two. By the end of the day Mery counted that three hundred people had signed in and that fifteen of them would do presentations. It was past ten o'clock at night when the women finished their sums.

"Three hundred people," Samantha mumbled. "That's a little less than what I was hoping for."

"Well, we gave people a three-day deadline so they could sign in. Today was only the first day," Mery answered. "I'm sure more people will call tomorrow."

"Maybe you're right," Samantha said, biting the cap of her pen. "Well, I'm going home. Greg must be waiting for me to start dinner."

"See ya tomorrow," Mery said as her friend left the house.

Outside, Samantha looked to the sky and smiled. She started to walk toward her house when she bumped into Matt, who was coming from the opposite direction. He greeted his neighbor and apologized.

"Where are you off to?" Samantha asked.

"I'm going to Thales's house," Matt answered. "He needs to talk to me. I was supposed to go there last night, but I came home awfully late."

"Oh," Samantha said and smiled. "Well, I'm off to my house. See you later, Matt."

"See you."

Matt walked away and crossed the street. Once he reached his cousin's front porch, the boy rang the doorbell. Ana opened the door and gave her nephew a kiss. The boy walked upstairs and entered his cousin's bedroom.

"I'm sorry for not coming last night." Matt said as he closed the door behind him.

"That's fine," Thales answered, sitting on his bed.

"So—" Matt said, staring at his cousin, who looked nervous. "What did you wanna talk to me about?"

"Matt, you're my cousin and my best friend. So I believe that you are the only person I can rely on to tell this secret," Thales replied.

"Okay," Matt said, smiling nervously. "I'm a little freaked out right now. Did something happen?"

"Matt," Thales answered, "I'm gay."

~oOo~

Jack Stappord was standing in his office, looking out the window. Greendale was a beautiful city, but at night its beauty went to a whole different level. The moonlight would mix with the lights of the buildings, creating a magnificent effect. When he heard someone knocking on his door, Jack turned around. Bill entered the office and sat by the table. The businessman put his whiskey glass on the counter next to the window and said, "You've failed."

"Jack," Bill said, shaking, "I am so sorry."

"You shot the mayor's wife!" Jack yelled, punching the wall. "Which, by the way, is completely different from Samantha!"

"I know," Bill answered. "But she stood in the way right as I shot! It's not my fault!"

"I have to do things slowly now," Jack said, itching his chin. "Gregory and Samantha cannot suspect I'm on the move."

"I could—"

"You could keep your mouth shut and stop fucking up my plans!" Jack yelled, staring at his associate. "I am sick of your mistakes!"

"Jack, if you don't like my work, why don't you do it yourself?" Bill replied, standing up. "I can't stand this couple hunt of yours anymore!"

The man walked toward the door but turned around when he heard a noise. Jack was leaning against his table.

"I have yet to dismiss you," Jack said softly.

"You don't dismiss me anymore," Bill answered. "I don't work for you anymore, Jack."

"Fine," Stappord replied. "I knew this day would come … sadly."

Bill turned around again but stopped. He touched the doorknob but glanced at Jack for a second and asked, "What do you even want with them?"

"Gregory Desmond took something from me," Jack explained, grabbing his whiskey glass. "And Samantha must pay for leaving me."

Bill, the ragged subordinate, let go of the doorknob and returned to his seat. Jack Stappord poured more whiskey in his glass and gave another glass of the drink to his associate. Bill sipped twice and made a disgusted face but kept on drinking.

Jack looked out the window one more time and decided to sit down. The men were quiet with their own thoughts until Bill said:

"So you're seeking revenge? Gregory took your woman, and now you want them dead."

"Things are not quite that simple, mate," Jack answered. "I don't want just revenge, I also want protection."

"Protection?" Bill said and laughed, spreading his horrible breath through the air. "Why in the world would a man like you need fucking protection?"

"We all need protection, Bill," Jack said. "That's the universal need. The only difference is the reason why people need protection."

"Really? And what would those reasons be?"

"Many reasons!" the businessman said. "One could need safety … or hiding a secret, while others need it for some more serious motives, which is my case."

"And why is your case serious?" Bill asked.

"Actually," Jack said, standing up, "I need protection for many reasons. Let's just say things happen to people who do business with me sometimes. And I cannot let my extracurricular activities be discovered, even though there has been some investigation of them already."

"What do you mean by *things happen with people*?" Bill asked and took a huge sip of his whiskey.

"Oh, c'mon now, Bill!" Jack said and laughed. "You kill people for a living! A lot of things that happened to people happened because of you! You know that."

"So what?" Bill asked when he finally realized what was going on. "Those deaths cannot be traced back to me. Have you seen how many cases were closed because they couldn't find the killer?"

"Or to me—" Jack said, holding a letter opener. "I make sure to get rid of any loose ends that might tie me to the murders."

"But people know you, Jack!" Bill said in disbelief.

"People know Jack Stappord, executive and philanthropist. But they don't know Jack Stappord, leader of the Greendale and Los Angeles underworld of crime."

"Do you actually think that in a city like ours people wouldn't suspect you?" Bill asked as he stood up.

"I'm sure they suspect something, but nothing concrete," Jack answered. "Like I said before, there were some investigations, but buying people off is not hard these days."

"You're gonna fall into your own lie, Jack. But I won't go down with you. Don't worry. You're secret is safe with me, but I'm out!"

"I know you are," Jack said, walking toward his friend. "You've been out for a long time."

In that moment Jack raised his arm and stabbed Bill's neck with the letter opener. The ragged man stifled a scream as he fell down on the floor with blood dripping from his throat. Jack stared at his friend and saw his blood pooling into a red pond on the carpet.

"I am so sorry, my friend. But that had to be done."

Jack turned around and grabbed the whiskey bottle. He poured the drink on the floor and threw the bottle away once it was empty. The executive got a lighter from his pocket and lit the flame.

"Jack Stappord is no longer."

~oOo~

Matt sat on his cousin's bed while Thales walked back and forth around the room.

"Did you tell anybody else?" Matt asked.

"No, just you," Thales answered. "Who else could I tell? I've got no one else."

"Your mother?"

"No!" Thales said nervously. "She cannot know. Please promise me you won't tell a soul about this."

"I promise," Matt said, standing up. "And I am proud of you for coming out, even if it's just to me. I gotta go now."

"Thanks. And don't forget. You made a promise."

"I won't break it."

~oOo~

The next day Carlota Mackenzie got a phone call from David Thompson telling her that Diane was finally able to go home. Carlota left her house and drove down to the mayor's home with the intention of meeting with her friend, who greeted her with open arms.

"Carlota, I am so sorry for what I've done!" Diane said.

"You don't have to apologize, dear," Carlota answered. "I know how our husband's business can affect our lives. But the only thing that matters now is that you are okay."

"Thank you," Diane said. "Now let's talk about my party. Are you coming?"

"Yes, I am," Carlota replied. "You just have to tell me the date. Since you just got out of the hospital, I imagine you won't be able to attend your ball on the scheduled day."

"Don't be ridiculous! Of course I'll attend the ball. Nothing will be changed."

David's phone rang. He left the living room and went to the kitchen to take his phone call.

"Hello?" he said. "Michelle, I can't talk right now. Diane just came home from the hospital, and we have a visitor. I gotta give them some attention. No, I did not forget about our date tonight. Yes, the hotel is confirmed. All right. I love you too. Bye."

Once he hung up the phone, David turned around to leave the kitchen, but he was startled when he saw Carlota standing right at the door. Carlota smiled at her friend, and he gave an embarrassed smile. David left the kitchen as Carlota walked inside.

A few moments later, Carlotta came back to the living room, holding a glass of water that she handed to Diane. Carlota turned her head only to see David staring at her. She raised an eyebrow as he quickly looked away.

The three friends kept chatting for a couple of hours more until Diane decided it was time for a bath. She went up the stairs and yelled good-bye to Carlota.

"I'll be right up, honey," David said as he heard Diane entering their room.

"Well, David, this was a pleasant afternoon," Carlota said. "I'll call you later to check on her."

"Of course, Carlota. Thank you," David said. "But before you go, I'd like to ask you a question."

"Sure. Ask away."

"When you were in the kitchen, did you happen to listen to my phone call?" he asked.

"No," she answered, "when I arrived at the kitchen, you had just finished the call. Why?"

"Nothing much," David answered. "It's just that I feel uncomfortable when people listen to my phone calls."

"Well," Carlota said and smiled. "Don't worry. I didn't hear anything. See you later, David."

~oOo~

Samantha closed the file and put the object on the chair that was right next to her. Mery poured some tea in a cup and gave it to her friend and then served herself. The blonde tasted the drink and said, "Today was a very tiring day."

"For you or for me?" Mery asked and laughed. "I sold more tickets and registered more people. This is going to be a big event."

"Oh, thank goodness!" Samantha said in excitement. "I needed to do something like that to take my mind off other stuff."

"What other stuff?" Mery asked, raising an eyebrow.

"Nothing," Samantha said and sighed. "Shall we continue? So, I think we should split the event."

"I was thinking the exact same thing today," Mery replied. "We could split the event over two days."

"That was my thought. The only problem is the medals."

"It's not that big of a deal. We'll just ask the company to make more," Mery said. "Instead of three we'll order six. And it's not gonna be that expensive. And about the contestants, we'll just put ten on the first day and ten on the second since we have twenty of them."

"Then why six medals?" Samantha asked.

"Because like that, we could reward six winners," Mery explained. "The best three of the first day and the best three of the second day. It would be much more dynamic."

Samantha smiled and nodded. She wrote Mery's ideas on a piece of paper and was quiet for a moment.

"But what about the people? Are we changing the tickets?" Samantha asked finally.

"I don't think it's necessary. People will have the chance to watch all twenty of the presentations," Mery concluded.

"Interesting. I guess this might work."

"Not might," Mery replied. "It will work."

"I like your determination, Mery," Samantha said. "Okay … I guess it's time for us to call it a day! Tomorrow I'll bring the flyers with the new dates to the printers."

"Perfect!"

~oOo~

Carla was standing in front of the mirror on the dresser, putting lipstick on her lips. Matt sat on his mother's bed, playing on his phone. He stopped for a second and glanced at his mother.

"What are you doing?" he asked. "You're going to a restaurant, not to a whore house."

"What?" Carla said, staring at her son.

"You're wearing way too much makeup. You look like a clown … or worse than that," the boy said as he stood up. "You gotta relax."

"I can't!" Carla said. "I am really nervous! But I'll try to relax and give a good impression."

"Good."

Carla walked into the bathroom and closed the door. She came back a few moments later wearing much less makeup. Matt smiled and nodded positively to his mother. Carla approached the dresser again and started to comb her hair.

"I'm ready," she said.

"You look great," the boy said.

"Thanks … and while I'm out, what will you be doing?"

"Sarah's coming over."

"Is she sleeping here?" Carla asked, putting on her earrings.

"Probably."

"Does Sheila know?"

"Yes," Matt answered.

Carla nodded and put on some rings. She looked at her reflection in the mirror and smiled. Matt came closer to his mother and said, "You should go downstairs. He might arrive at any second now."

When Matt finished his sentence, the doorbell rang. Carla shrugged and looked at her son. The boy touched his mother's shoulders and said, "Go. Relax. You're beautiful, and a really nice person. Everything will be fine."

"I hope so."

~oOo~

When the doorbell rang, Carlota took a few minutes to open the door since she was just finishing to unmold a cake. When she put the dessert on a tray, she went to receive her guest. When she opened the door, the mayor was standing outside.

"David?" Carlota asked. "What are you doing here?"

"We need to talk," he said.

"Don't you think it's a little late for a conversation?" Carlota asked.

"No," he replied. "Besides, I don't plan to take long."

Carlota raised an eyebrow and allowed the mayor to walk inside. She closed the door and followed him to the kitchen. He sat at the counter while the Mackenzie matriarch grabbed two Coca-Cola cans from the fridge. She went back and sat in front of her friend.

"I just unmolded a cake. Do you want a piece?" she asked.

"No, just the Coke is fine," he answered.

"So—" Carlota said. "What do we have to talk about that is so important you couldn't wait till tomorrow?"

"Carlota, how long have we known each other?"

"I don't know," she answered. "A really long time. Like thirty, thirty-five years."

"That really is a long time. That's why I think I know when you're lying."

"Lying? What do you mean by that?"

"You know what I'm talking about," David said and laughed. "You heard my phone call this morning."

Carlota raised an eyebrow but said nothing. David was looking at her with a mischievous smile on his face. Both were quiet for several minutes. David hoped that his friend was making up an excuse, but instead Carlota answered something he did not expect, "Yes, I did listen to your conversation this morning."

"Aren't you going to deny it again?" David asked as his smile faded away.

"No," Carlota replied, "I lied this morning as a matter of respect to Diane."

"Oh … right."

"You're cheating on your wife, David. For how long?"

"A couple of months," he answered. "Michelle is my secretary, but Diane doesn't suspect anything. And … you're not telling her."

"Oh—" Carlota said and scowled as she drank her Coke. "Don't count on that, my dear. Diane is my best friend, and I won't let her suffer like that. I think it's getting late, and I believe you know your way to the door."

Carlota stood up and walked toward the door. When he was about to leave the room, David said, "If you ruin my marriage, I guess I'll have to ruin your friendship!"

"What do you mean by that?" Carlota asked, turning around to face the mayor.

"If you tell Diane about my affair, I guess I'll have to tell her about our little adventure years ago."

"You wouldn't do that!" Carlota said.

"Oh yes, I would."

"But that was ages ago. My husband had just died, and I was drunk!" Carlota replied.

"Yes, you were ... on the first night," David replied. "But what about the other months?"

"You son of a bitch," Carlota said. "Bastard."

"Well," David answered, standing up. "It's getting late. Go to bed. I know my way to the door."

David blinked at his *friend* and left the room. Carlota sat on a chair by the table and punched the wall next to her. The tears of rage streamed down her face as she thought of a solution to her problem.

~oOo~

The restaurant, although crowded, was a really nice place. The tables were organized in a way that the place had more space for people to walk through. The low illumination and soft music made that ambience a little bit more romantic and charming.

Carla and her new friend, Clark, sat right on the center of the hall. They shared a bottle of wine, while they enjoyed a plate of cheese, ham, olives, and other appetizers. The couple couldn't stop laughing about the way they had met at the coffee shop.

"Well, I'm happy that we're doing this," Carla said. "Our first encounters were absolutely dreadful. And yet you were able to give me a nice impression."

"Well," Clark said, "I try my best whenever I meet a beautiful woman."

"Oh … thank you," Carla answered. "Could you excuse me for bit? I gotta go to the restroom."

Clark shook his head with a smile. Carla stood up and walked to the restroom. When she came back to the dining hall, she noticed that Clark was talking to a man. She approached her friend and asked, "Hey, Clark, aren't you going to introduce me to your friend?"

"Hello, Carla," the man said.

"Carla, would you please tell me who this guy is?" Clark asked.

Carla was in shock. The fact that she was staring at that man after so many years didn't please her. She could feel the rage taking over her body and the sadness and old memories coming back.

"Oh my God, what are you doing here?" Carla asked.

"I came to see you," the man said. "But as I can see, you already got over me."

"You left me with a baby, Robert!" Carla replied. "After the day you left, I swore that I'd never talk to you again!"

"Wait, Matt's his son?" Clark asked. "So you're the son of a bitch that abandoned his own child?"

"Hey, who the fuck do you think you are to meddle?" Robert asked. "You're not a part of the family."

"He might not be family, but hell knows you're not either!" Carla said. "Now go away and leave me the fuck alone."

"I'll go," Robert said, walking away, "but we will meet again."

~oOo~

Gregory was sitting on the couch when he heard Samantha calling for him from the kitchen. He stood up and walked toward the door, but he stopped when something on the news caught his attention. He returned to the living room and turned up the TV volume.

"A fire that took the life of the famous executive Jack Stappord," the news reporter said.

"Samantha!" Gregory yelled. "Get over here!"

"What happened?" Samantha asked as she came running to the living room.

"Look!" Gregory said, pointing at the TV.

Samantha's eyes were filled with tears. She screamed in happiness and hugged her husband, who started to laugh in pure excitement. The couple stared at each other, and then they kissed passionately.

"Finally," Samantha said, "I can stop my lying."

"We're free!" Greg said. "Jack Stappord is dead!"

"Let's have dinner," Samantha said. "Let's open that bottle of champagne to celebrate!"

~oOo~

Clark got back home a few moments after eleven. He hung his coat on the hanger next to the door and turned on the lights. When he reached the living room, there was a woman sitting on the couch. She was a tall redhead, and she was extremely beautiful. She stood up and greeted Clark.

"Here's your dinner," he said, handing her a little box from the restaurant.

"Thanks," the woman said. "And how was the date?"

"It was good," Clark answered. "She's a nice girl. Perfect—"

"That's great. Did you drink?"

"Yes."

"Well, the next time you take her out, don't drink."

"Adriana, I believe I pay you to mop the floors, not to give me orders," Clark said, looking at his maid.

"Indeed," Adriana replied. "But I know that when you drink, you can't shut up. What would happen if your friend found out about your dirty secret?"

Clark faced his maid with fury. But Adriana maintained her neutral facial expression. Both stared at each other for a moment when he said at last, "If you tell her anything—"

"Don't worry about me. I won't tell anything," Adriana said. "But if you keep drinking, someone will find out."

"No, they won't!" Clark said.

"Oh, they will," Adriana replied. "Remember, Clark, when the alcohol's poured, the secrets come out of the bottle. Thanks for bringing my dinner."

Adriana smiled and walked away. Clark stood in the living room for a long time before he went to his bedroom. Once on his bed, he couldn't sleep. He could only see her face—his sister's face, that is.

"Susan," he said.

CHAPTER

4

A Surprising Encounter

IT WAS THE EVE OF Samantha's talent show and things at Crystal Street couldn't be busier. Electricians and mechanics were installing the equipment for the next day's event, while Mery and Samantha supervised the organization, keeping an eye on every flaw they could find.

Besides that, the residents of Crystal Street were all very excited with the event. After all, Samantha's parties were always the best back in the day. And now that she was back, they were all expecting something bigger!

"So that's where the stage is gonna be?" Matt asked as he met his aunt on the street.

"Yes," Mery answered with a smile, "the show is gonna be a success, especially Thales's presentation."

"Thales's performing?" Matt asked.

"Yup," Mery said, clapping her hands. "He's gonna read a poem. And instead of reading it, he's gonna sing it. It's a beautiful performance, although I wasn't able to understand what he meant on a few parts."

"Oh, crap."

"What?"

"Umm, nothing," Matt said, walking away. "Good luck to you two!"

"Crazy kid," Mery said.

"Who's crazy?" Samantha asked, approaching her friend.

"Matt, but not on the pejorative way," Mery explained. "But I just had the weirdest conversation with him."

"Boys that age are weird," Samantha replied. "They can only think about sex."

"Well, I am no teenager, but I still think about sex all the time," Mery said and laughed.

"And who doesn't?" Samantha said.

~oOo~

The doorbell rang, and Ana opened the door. Matt greeted his aunt and entered the house. The boy ran to his cousin's room and locked the door once he went inside. Thales stood up from his bed and asked, "What happened?"

"You're singing a poem?" Matt asked in return.

"Yes."

"And you performed it to Aunt Mery? And what's in that poem? Did you confess what you told me the other day?"

"Kinda," Thales replied, embarrassed.

"Thales, my God!" Matt said. "Did you think about what will happen if your mother understands what you mean? Why would you do this?"

"Yes, I have, but I gotta tell someone," Thales said.

"And your idea is to tell the whole street?" Matt asked. "You told me, Thales. I am your best friend. When it's time to tell your mother, I will be there as well as when you tell the rest of the family."

"But I feel comfortable with the poem idea," Thales explained.

"Hear me out," Matt began. "Tell Samantha you'd rather sing on the second day. That will give you one day more to think about what I told you."

"But Matt—" Thales protested.

"Do what I say. Trust me."

~oOo~

Helena was at the kitchen counter slicing some carrots when her phone rang. She quickly washed her hands and answered the call.

"Hello?"

"Helena Trevers?"

"This is she," Helena answered.

"This is John Smith. I'm calling to say we don't need your services anymore. The product you have with you, keep or sell it … because you are no longer needed."

"What?" Helena said, perplexed. "Why don't you need me anymore? Did I do something wrong?"

"No … but the boss is dead. They've caught him," John replied. "The business is done."

Helena let the phone fall on the floor, and once it hit the ground, it broke into pieces. She sat on a chair and touched her chest with shaken hands. The tears started to run down her rosy cheeks.

A few minutes later she stood up and walked to the fridge, where she got a bottle of *Chateau Margaux* and removed the cork. Instead of getting a glass, Helena decided to drink it out of the bottle.

Hours later she had already drunk three bottles of wine and one of vodka. Some of the bottles laid broken on the floor next to Helena, who was starting to pass out, completely drunk.

"Why? I don't understand," she said while she slowly sat up.

She grabbed a whiskey bottle that sat next to her. She drank the whole bottle in a matter of seconds and threw the empty object against the wall. The woman held on to the counter and pulled herself up.

"They … they'll … pay for this," she stammered.

When she finished her sentence, Helena just fell to the ground and passed out.

~oOo~

David Thompson sat behind his desk at his office when someone entered the room. The lady was slim with hair as dark as ebony. Her eyes were of a blue so intense that a lot of people would say they were actually purple. She came closer to the mayor and handed him a file.

"Thank you," he said as he grabbed the file.

"David," the lady said, "we still haven't had the chance to talk about your strange behavior at the hotel the other day."

"Strange behavior?" he asked without taking his eyes off the papers he was working on.

"Yes, well … you seemed off. Did something happen?"

"A lot of things happened, Michelle," the mayor said finally, staring at his secretary.

"Oh, my darling," Michelle said as she walked around the table to massage her boss's shoulders. "You ought to tell me. What's bothering you?"

David stood up and walked to the other side of his office. He poured himself a glass of whiskey and went back to his desk but did not sit down. The mayor sipped his drink two times before he continued, "Diane has a friend named Carlota. They are very close, practically sisters."

"And that bothers you?" Michelle asked.

"Not at all," David answered. "But Carlota knows about us, you and me."

"What?" Michelle asked in shock. "But how?"

"She heard—by accident—our phone call the other day," David explained. "And now she plans to tell my wife."

"Oh my God, David! What are we gonna do?"

"I blackmailed her," David said. "But I've known Carlota for years. She's a tough woman. She won't give in to blackmail. And Diane will believe her word, no matter what I say."

"So what?" Michelle asked; "We have to do something!"

"I know exactly what to do," David replied. "You are fired, and our adventures are over."

"What?" Michelle asked with tears in her eyes. "David, you don't mean that."

"Yes, I do. I will not let my marriage end because of you!"

"But it's this Carlota! She's the one who's gonna ruin your life!" Michelle protested. "Don't do this, David!"

"However, it's easier to blame the lover than the best friend," David replied. "Besides, you are just a secretary. I think people will just believe that you are not a good one. That's why you got fired. Isn't that the perfect alibi?"

"David—" Michelle said, sobbing.

"Pack your things and go."

Michelle stood there for a moment, hoping that her love would deny everything he had just said, but her prayers were not answered. She ran toward the door as she cried in complete disbelief. When she left the room, Michelle shut the door with such rage that two pictures fell to the ground.

~oOo~

Clark sat at the head of the table while Matt and Carla took the seats next to him. Adriana, the maid, served a delicious boneless chicken for lunch, accompanied by some vegetables and well-made mashed potatoes.

"The food's great!" Carla said with a smile.

"Everything is perfect," Matt agreed.

"I'm glad you all like it," Adriana said. "Would you like something to drink? Water? Juice? A soft drink? Or maybe a good wine?"

Clark glanced at his maid. She smiled her devious smile as she waited for the guests' answers.

"Matt's not old enough to drink. Why don't you bring us some juice?" Clark said instead.

"Fine," Adriana replied. "I'll be right back."

After lunch they went to the living room in order to talk and to get to know one another better. A few moments later, Adriana came in the room carrying a tray with a teapot and some cups.

"Shall I pour the coffee?"

"No, Adriana, thank you," Clark said. "I'll take care of it."

"You're welcome," Adriana said, turning around.

"Umm, Clark, could you excuse me for a bit. I've gotta use the restroom," Matt said.

"Come with me, Matt," Adriana said. "The toilet down here is broken. I'll take you upstairs."

The boy smiled and stood up. He followed Adriana to the second floor, where they walked to the end of the corridor and turned left. She opened one of the doors and revealed a ginormous suite.

"You can use the bathroom in here," Adriana said.

"Are you sure? This seems to be somebody's room," Matt asked.

"Don't worry. This room hasn't been used for years now."

"Oh—"

Matt entered and went straight to the bathroom. He locked the door and pulled his pants down in order to pee. Once he was done, he pulled his pants up and flushed the toilet. When the boy finished washing his hands, he started to look for paper towels so he could dry himself, but there was nothing in sight.

"Crap," he said.

He opened the cabinet under the sink, looking for some paper towels, but what he found was rather unusual. Matt got one of the white bricks he found in the cabinet and analyzed its content. There was a white powder that resembled wheat. But Matt was sure about what it actually was.

"Oh my God—"

"Matt?" Adriana asked, knocking on the door. "Are you okay?"

"Umm," the boy said nervously. "Yeah! Everything is fine. I'll be right out."

Matt threw the cocaine brick inside the cabinet and closed the doors. When he left the bathroom, Adriana was waiting for him outside with a towel.

"Sorry, I forgot to give you this."

"Oh … I looked for one but couldn't find it," he said while he dried his hands. "Thanks."

"You're welcome," Adriana said as she got the towel back. "Now go downstairs. I'll put this in the bathroom."

Matt shook his head and walked outside, but before he was able to leave the room, the maid called for him. He turned around to face the woman and smiled.

"Are you sure that everything is okay?"

"Yeah," he answered, walking away.

Adriana shrugged and entered the bathroom. She hung the towel on a little hook next to the sink and left. When she reached the bedroom's door, she stopped. The maid looked at the corridor and then to the bathroom, realizing her mistake.

Adriana ran toward the bathroom and kneeled in front of the cabinet. When she opened the doors, the bricks were all messed up. Adriana closed the doors and ran back outside. Once she reached the middle of the stairs, Matt was already in his seat, but he was staring oddly at his mother's friend.

The boy grabbed his cup of coffee and took a sip. When he put his cup down, Matt looked to the staircase and his eyes met Adriana's. He kept staring at her and made a small gesture with his head. The maid raised an eyebrow and nodded subtly. Matt widened his eyes and glanced at his mother's friend.

"Matt?"

"I'm sorry. What?" the boy asked.

"Are you okay?" Clark asked. "You look pale."

"Oh, yeah. I'm okay," Matt answered. "Don't worry about me."

~oOo~

Thales rang the doorbell and waited a few minutes until someone opened the door. Gregory Desmond greeted him and asked him to go inside. The boy smiled and followed his neighbor to the living room.

"What can I do to help you, Thales?"

"I'd like to speak with Samantha," he answered.

"She's not home yet. She left with Mery to run some errands for the talent show," Gregory explained.

"Oh," Thales answered, a little saddened. "Okay, well … I'll come back later."

"Are you sure? I might be able to help you."

"I don't know. I might as well just wait for her."

"If you insist," Gregory said with a smile.

He walked the boy to the front door. Once in the hall, Thales turned to his neighbor and thanked him.

"You're welcome!" Gregory replied.

Thales smiled and turned around to exit the house, but a shiny object caught his attention. The boy looked carefully and noticed the CIA badge on the counter next to the door. The badge had Gregory's name on it.

"Gregory, you're a prosecutor, right?"

"Yes, I am," the man answered. "Why?"

"Umm … nothing important. But I might have to do an assignment for school, and you might be useful."

"But we're in the middle of the summer," Gregory said.

"Yes," Thales said. "That's why I said maybe. My teacher will explain the assignment to us once classes start again."

"Got it," Gregory said. "Well, if you need help, just call me."

"I will."

~oOo~

Matt and Carla spent the weekend at Clark's house. Matt decided it was time to snoop around, looking for clues into his host's life. When his mom and Clark left for the movies, Matt took the opportunity to chat with Adriana.

The redheaded maid was making pudding in the kitchen when Matt entered the room. She glanced at him for a second, but she soon looked away. Matt sat at the counter and waited a few minutes to talk, but Adriana was the one who started the conversation:

"You've probably come to ask me about the *bricks* you found in the bathroom."

"Bingo!" Matt said.

"And now you're asking yourself if those bricks belong to Clark."

"You're two for two!" Matt said. "Except I am sure those bricks belong to Clark because you confirmed it to me earlier today."

"Did I?" Adriana asked as she mixed the creamy mixture.

"Yes," Matt answered, observing the woman. "When I looked at him right after finding the bricks, I looked at you, and you nodded to me."

"And you took that as a confirmation?" Adriana said and laughed. "Then you must be rather stupid."

The maid turned off the stove and grabbed a pan that was next to the sink. She poured the mixture into it and put the object in the oven. After she set the timer on the appliance, she stared at Matt.

"What do you mean?" he asked.

"I mean that you are too young to understand certain things," Adriana said as she walked toward the kitchen door.

"Adriana!" Matt called, running after her. "I mean it! I need to know if this man is an addict!"

"What difference will it make?" she asked.

"He's dating my mother!" Matt replied. "And I have the right to protect her. Wouldn't you like to protect your parents if something happened to them?"

"Yes!" Adriana said. "My father died because I couldn't protect him. Weeks later my mom also died because I failed her too."

"Oh my God, Adriana, I had no idea. I'm so sorry," Matt said.

"Like I said, you're way too young to understand stuff," the maid replied. "Don't stick your nose where it doesn't belong, Matt. You might put yourself in danger."

"Adriana, wait," the boy said.

"What?" she asked, facing Matt.

"Why don't you use your parents' death as a reason to help me? You couldn't protect them, but you can help me protect my mother."

"Because that won't bring them back," Adriana said as she walked away.

~oOo~

When Mery opened the door, she encountered Thales standing outside. She permitted her nephew to enter her home, and both went to the kitchen, where Mery was fixing dinner. She turned off the stove and sat at the table with her nephew.

"What can I do for you?"

"Umm … I went to Samantha's house today," Thales explained.

"To do what?"

"Well, I wanted to tell her I am not performing tomorrow, but she wasn't home."

"Wait, what? Why aren't you performing tomorrow? Did something happen?" Mery asked, raising an eyebrow.

"Because I need to think."

"Think?"

"This is subject for later," the boy said. "So when I got to Samantha's, Gregory received me 'cause she wasn't there. And when I was leaving—"

"What happened?"

"I think they're lying to us."

"Lying to us?" Mery asked. "What do you mean by that?"

"I don't think Gregory is a real prosecutor," Thales said. "When I was leaving their house, I found this badge with Greg's name on it. I think he's a CIA agent."

Mery was so shocked she dropped the knife on the floor. She stared at her nephew for a little while, trying to find the courage to carry on the conversation.

"Are you sure?"

"Absolutely sure," he said. "But why would they hide this from us?"

"My dear nephew, this is a question that will be answered very soon," Mery said. "Count on that."

~oOo~

David and Carlota sat at the center of the restaurant. They shared a bottle of wine while they discussed the recent events of their relationship, which had gone from friendly to blackmail.

"Look, David. I did not come here to share wine with you, and I'm pretty sure that this was not the reason you invited me either."

"Yes," he answered. "I brought you here because I want you to know that my affair with Michelle has ended."

"Oh," Carlota said. "And that was news that you had to deliver in person? Seriously, you could have called. It would have saved me the trouble to look at your face. Like it's not enough to wake up with you on the front page every day."

"Ha! I love your sense of humor, Carlota!" David laughed hysterically. "I don't know how I was able to walk away from you! I'm glad we are close again."

"First of all," Carlota explained, "I did not make a joke. Second of all, I am not close to you. I'm close to your wife."

The waiter arrived with their orders that were made minutes ago. When the man walked away, David tasted his wine and said, "You know, I wouldn't mind starting another intimate relationship with you."

"Then you'd have to learn how to resuscitate yourself because if you touch me, I'll stab you with my fork," Carlota said.

"Carlota, don't make threats, even if they're not for real," David said. "You're not in that position."

"And you are not in the position to make indecent proposals!"

Carlota stood up and threw the contents of her glass on David's shirt. The mayor widened his eyes in shock. He stood up and looked around only to realize that everyone was staring at them.

"Have you lost your mind?"

"No, and before I lose it for real, I'll go home! Enjoy your fucking dinner."

Carlota grabbed her purse and walked away. Once outside, she gave her ticket to the valet so he could pick her car up for her. While she was waiting for her vehicle to arrive, Carlota stood there, observing the people who came in and out of the restaurant, waiting for the mayor to come after her, but there was no sign of him.

Minutes later the valet returned and approached Carlota.

"Carlota Mackenzie?" he asked.

"Yes."

"Here's your car, ma'am."

"Oh, thank you," she said.

Carlota got her car keys and walked to her car as the valet returned to his post. Before she went around the car, she stopped when someone touched her shoulder. Before she turned around, Carlota thought she would find David standing behind her;

however, she was wrong. When she turned around, Carlota met one of the girls who had just arrived at the restaurant, and she was standing in front of her now.

"Your name is Carlota?"

"Who's asking?" Carlota asked with curiosity.

"I am Michelle. I think you know who I am."

"Oh yes … Michelle," Carlota answered with a smile. "The mayor's lover. I must say I was surprised when I learned your age."

"And why is that?" Michelle asked.

"Because I never thought David could relate to woman that young. And here I am dying to ask you the main question. What do you want?"

"I want to know why you were gonna tell on us to that old hag Diane!"

"Hag?" Carlota felt her blood boil. "Listen, you little bitch. Diane is a lovely woman—"

In that moment the restaurant's doors opened, and David walked toward Carlota. He was furious like no one had ever seen before.

"Carlota!" he yelled.

"Oh fuck," Carlota mumbled.

"Are you two here together?" Michelle asked, horrified.

"Michelle?" David asked. "What are you doing here?"

"No, what are you doing here with this woman?"

"Hey!" Carlota said, pushing Michelle away. "I am not just any woman!"

"Carlota!" David said. "Now you have lost it!"

"No, David!" Carlota yelled. "I am just pissed. With you, her, and myself! She acts like she's better than everyone, but she came out of the same sewer we did. The same den of lying, cheating bastards!"

Carlota was furious. If her blood was boiling before, it was not even close to how she was at this particular moment.

"I am trying to protect my marriage!" David said.

"And I am trying to protect my friendship!"

"Who's trying to protect me?" Michelle asked. "David?"

David and Carlota stared at the secretary. The mayor glanced at Carlota, who snorted with rage. Her eyes were red, and a tear was running down her face. David closed his eyes and took a deep breath. He turned to Michelle and said, "No one is trying to protect you because you mean nothing to anyone."

"David—"

"Go away and get out of my life just like I told you to do."

"You don't mean that!" Michelle said and sobbed.

"I said, 'Get out my life!'" David replied. "You were a bad experience that I don't want to remember."

"But you said you loved me!" Michelle said.

"He lied," Carlota said. "Just like the other men that cheat."

"Exactly," he said.

Michelle stared at them one last time and ran away in tears. Carlota shook her head and turned her back to the mayor. David tried holding her, but she shrugged off his grip.

"Just leave me be, David."

"Carlota."

"No more talking! I've had enough stress for one night. That's enough."

Carlota dried her eyes and entered her car and then drove away. David stared at the street for a couple of seconds, and then he handed his ticket to the valet.

CHAPTER
5

The Talent Show

CARLOTA PARKED HER CAR IN the driveway and walked to her house once she stepped out of the vehicle. When she was about to unlock the front door, Carlota heard a noise. She turned around to investigate and spotted Helena lying in the gutter. The matriarch of the Mackenzie family ran toward her friend, preoccupied and confused.

"Helena, honey, is everything okay?"

"Yeah," Helena stammered.

"Oh my God," Carlota said, covering her nose. "Have you been drinking?"

"Just a bit. I wa-was ta-ta-taking out the tra-trash."

Carlota raised an eyebrow and walked back to check the trash can. She found fifteen wine bottles, three vodka bottles, and two whiskey bottles, all completely empty. She turned to her friend and realized Helena was not okay, not one bit.

"C'mon, sweetie. Up you go," Carlota said, pulling Helena up. "Put your arms around me. I'm taking you to bed."

They took a long while to go up the stairs because of Helena's condition. When they finally got to the main bedroom, Carlota put her friend on the bed. Helena thanked her and covered herself with the sheets.

"Stay here. I'll be right back with a pill and a glass of water for you."

"Okay."

Carlota went to the kitchen. She got the glass of water and an aspirin and went back to her friend's room. After Helena took her medicine, Carlota went to the bathroom and started to look for a towel.

"Helena, where do you keep your towels?"

"In the chiffonier here in the bedroom," Helena answered.

Carlota returned from the bathroom and opened the top drawer of the bureau, but she didn't find towels. What Carlota found was something much more *interesting* than towels.

"Helena, my God," Carlota said, facing her friend.

"What happened?" Helena asked as she sat up on the bed.

"Would you like to explain this to me?" Carlota asked, throwing small cocaine packages at her friend's bed. "Is that why you've been drinking? Yes, I saw the bottles in your trash can."

"And what do you care?" Helena replied. "You, any of you—you never care about me! I'm always in the background, especially after Samantha returned."

"Cut the bullshit, Helena! This is serious!"

"You know what? I don't have to explain myself to anyone, especially you. Get out of my house! Out, out!"

Carlota rolled her eyes and left. It was when she heard the front door closing that Helena yelled. Her feelings were mixed up, probably an effect of the drinks she had earlier that night. Helena stayed quiet for a few minutes until her eyes found the little bag Carlota threw at her moments ago. And that's how Helena decided to try something new—one little bag, two little bags, three little bags.

~oOo~

When David got home, he hung his clothes on the hanger right next to the door. He put his car keys on the counter next to the hanger and walked to the living room. Once he got there, he saw something that really surprised him. Diane and Michelle were sitting on the couch.

"Hello, David," Diane said with a challenging tone. "Would you like to sit down?"

"Michelle?" he asked. "What are you doing here?"

"I had a little talk with your wife," Michelle answered. "Believe me, she wasn't happy."

"Diane—"

"Shut the hell up, you bastard!" Diane shouted. "I want you out of this house by tomorrow."

"See?" Michelle said and laughed. "She isn't happy at all."

"As for you, you fucking whore, I want you out right now!" Diane yelled.

"Fucking whore?" Michelle asked. "I did you a favor, you old hag."

"Old hag is that bitch mother of yours!" Diane said as she punched Michelle in the face.

Michelle fell to the floor, her nose bleeding.

"Really nice punch for an old hag, right?" Diane said. "Get this woman out of my house, David. Now!"

David nodded and helped Michelle up. He followed her outside and returned to his house, leaving his old lover behind. When the mayor walked in the living room, Diane was lying on the couch, helpless. David kneeled in front of his wife and held her hand.

"Honey, I am so sorry."

"What did I ever do wrong?" Diane said as she sobbed. "I spent all those years thinking I was the perfect wife, but you were having an affair with your secretary."

"But you are perfect."

"No, no, I'm not," Diane said and laughed. "And don't apologize. I made you unhappy all those years, so I should be the one apologizing. I am so very sorry."

"Let's go to our bedroom," David said. "We can talk about it there."

"You go," Diane answered. "I gotta be alone for a while."

David shook his head and walked up the stairs. Diane heard the bedroom door closing on the upper floor, and so she decided to sit down. She dried her tears and harrumphed.

"We'll talk about it, all right. I got big plans for you, bastard."

~oOo~

The following day, precisely at 10:00 a.m., a group of people arrived at Crystal Street. They were all there to witness the talent show Samantha was promoting. The street had never been as crowded, but it was for a good cause.

At eleven sharp Samantha took the stage. All of those people stood up and cheered for Samantha with great enthusiasm. Samantha cleared her throat and walked toward the microphone.

"Welcome!" she said. "First of all, I'd like to thank all of you for your presence. This is a very special day for me and for Marone's Orphanage, the place where all the money we collected here will be donated to! Now I want you all to be prepared to vote for the three best performances of the day! Ladies and gentlemen, our first performance—Laura Linley!"

A wave of applause sounded when Samantha left the stage, and little Laura took her place. The six-year-old violinist started to play her instrument and left everyone amazed with her grace and talent. While Samantha watched the girl's performance from backstage, she noticed Mery coming her way.

"Oh, Mery, there you are! I looked everywhere for you, I was starting to think that you had flaked."

"And why would I do that?" Mery asked. "I made you a promise, didn't I? And I keep my promises because I am no liar."

"Is everything okay?" Samantha asked. "You seem mad about something."

"Oh, no! Everything is fine! I'm all right."

"See, I think you're lying."

"Ah!" Mery laughed hysterically. "So you do know when people are lying?"

"What do you mean?" Samantha asked.

"Oh, don't play victim with me, Samantha. I know the truth!"

"Truth?" Samantha asked, astonished. "What truth?"

"You're blonde but not dumb!" Mery replied. "I know you've been lying to my family!"

Samantha couldn't understand what Mery meant by all those things, but she would soon. Before Samantha could answer, Laura Linley finished her performance, and the spectators all cheered. Samantha took the stage once again and announced the next performer. When she got to the backstage area, she pulled Mery to a corner.

"I still don't know what you mean. But for what it matters, I am not lying to you or your family."

"Cut the crap, Samantha!" Mery yelled. "I know Gregory works for the CIA!"

"What?" the blonde woman asked as she stepped back.

"Yes. Prosecutor you said? Prosecutor my ass! Why did you lie?"

"Mery," Samantha said with tears in her eyes.

"Why did you lie?" Mery shouted.

At that moment, Matt entered the backstage and ran toward the two women. His eyes widened.

"Have you two lost your minds? People can hear you screaming!" he said. "What's going on here?"

"Gregory is a CIA agent. That's what's going on," Mery answered without taking her eyes off Samantha.

"What?" Matt asked, looking at his neighbor.

"Yes, Samantha's been lying to us."

"Matt, Mery—"

"Why did you lie to us, Samantha?" Matt asked. "Oh, my goodness, I thought you were our friend!"

"I am your friend!" she said, sobbing.

"Then why did you lie?"

"Because he's a CIA agent, I can't go around telling people about that," Samantha answered.

"That's the worst lie I have ever heard," Mery replied. "I've met CIA agents before, and believe me, your story is a fake. My last boyfriend was CIA. So I'll leave you two options. Either you tell the truth, or our friendship is over."

~oOo~

While Matt, Mery, and Samantha discussed the fate of their friendship, another person tried to deal with another problem she had recently found out about.

She moved through the crowd till she found her daughters. Cordelia and Ana were cheering among the other people when they noticed their mother.

"I need your help!" Carlota said.

"With what?" Ana asked.

"Helena," Carlota explained. "I think she's become an alcoholic."

"What?" Cordelia asked. "How do you know that?"

"I found her last night lying in the gutter. I looked at her trash can, and I found more than fifteen bottles of booze."

"Oh God—"

"And then I found marijuana, cocaine, and something I thought was ecstasy in her bureau," Carlota said as she dried her forehead with her hand.

"Drugs?" Ana asked in shock. "What's going on with Helena? What happened next?"

"Then I confronted her, but she kicked me out. We gotta help her!"

"Yes, we do!" Cordelia said.

The three women started to walk back through the crowd to reach the other side of the street. When they finally reached Helena's house, Cordelia rang the doorbell, but no one answered. Ana called for her friend, but she got no answer either.

"Just kick down the door!" Carlota said. "It would be easier."

Ana was getting ready to kick the door when Cordelia turned the doorknob and the door slid opened. Carlota stared at her daughter for a second and entered the house. The place was a complete mess. There was broken glass everywhere, chairs lying on the floor, and an awful marijuana smell.

The three women ran to the second floor and got to their friend's bedroom, but the door was locked. Ana knocked a couple of times, but no one answered. Carlota pushed her daughters away and kicked the door in. The lock broke, and they could go inside.

"Very good," Ana said. "I didn't know you were that strong."

"Well, I'm old, but I take care of myself," Carlota replied as she walked in the bedroom.

The scene they saw was heartbreaking. Helena was lying on the bed with her head hanging next to the mattress as she drooled on the carpet. A vomit stain pooled under her head. Carlota and her daughters ran toward their friend, who was completely knocked out.

"She's not breathing," Ana said with tears in her eyes.

"Cordelia, call an ambulance … now!" Carlota said, pointing at her daughter.

~oOo~

Samantha was pushing through the crowd as Matt and Mery ran after her. Samantha tried to outwit her neighbors, but the anger they felt sharpened their senses. When she finally walked away from the crowd, Samantha started to run toward her house, but halfway there, Matt caught her by the arm.

"Let me go!" she said. "I don't have to explain myself to you!"

"Yes, you do!" Mery said, catching up with them.

"Samantha, we are friends," Matt said, letting go of his neighbor's arm. "How could you not trust us?"

"It's not a trusting issue," Samantha answered.

"Then what is it, Samantha?" Mery asked. "Please enlighten me because I sure don't understand why you lied to our faces!"

"I'm sorry," Samantha said. "I really am sorry."

"Seriously? That's all you can say to us now?" Matt asked.

"Yes."

"Unbelievable," Mery said and laughed. "So it is true what they say. Time changes people. And you, my friend, changed for the worst. We asked for the truth, but you wouldn't give it to us. Don't bother apologizing again. Our friendship is over."

"Good-bye, Samantha," Matt said.

Matt and his aunt turned around and walked away. Samantha started to cry and call for her friends, but neither of them turned around to see her. They just followed their path like nothing had happened.

~oOo~

Samantha's talent show was obfuscated that day by an ambulance that arrived at Crystal Street. The spectators of the event turned their attention to the paramedics that stopped right in front of Helena's house and entered in quite a hurry.

Minutes later Carlota Mackenzie and her two daughters, Ana and Cordelia, left the house in a state of complete shock. The paramedics came out a few moments later, carrying Helena on a rolling bed. As they put her in the ambulance, one of the paramedics approached Carlota.

"Which one of you is going with her?"

"I am," Carlota answered.

"No," Ana said, "I'll go. You stay here and rest, Mother. I'll get things done at the hospital. I'll call as soon as I get some news."

Ana said good-bye to her mother and sister and entered the vehicle. The medics turned the siren on, and the ambulance left the street. When the chaos ended, the spectators of the event decided it was time to leave, for the festivity spirit had faded away.

Once she was in her house, Carlota called the rest of her relatives and told them what had happened. A few moments later they were all gathered at her living room for more detailed information on the matter. When Carlota was done with her story, Matt and Mery agreed it was time to tell their relatives of another unpleasant story.

"What do you mean that she's not our friend anymore?"

"It means what it means," Mery replied. "She can't trust us."

"Yeah, Gregory is a CIA agent," Matt said. "Why couldn't she tell us that? And her excuse was beyond lame."

"Don't think you're overreacting a bit?" Cordelia asked. "There might be a story behind that."

"Exactly!" Carla said. "Mom's right. Are you going to end your friendship with Helena too because of what happened with her today?"

"That's different," Thales said. "Helena was under the influence of drugs and alcohol. She wasn't herself. There was no way she could hide this from us. Besides, she needed help, even though she didn't want any, but as we are good friends, we are here for her."

"Well, I agree with Matt and Mery," Carlota said. "Samantha lied, and we've known her for twenty freaking years. How could she not trust us enough to reveal a secret like that? That is not the attitude of a true friend."

At that moment, Carlota's phone rang. She let the machine answer. It was Ana calling from the hospital with news.

"How is she?" Carla asked once she pressed the button to put Ana on speaker.

"She's fine now," Ana answered. "She's in pain. That's why the doctors are keeping her on painkillers."

"Aren't those addictive?" Mery asked. "What good will that do? Stupid doctors."

"I tried to say that, but they kicked me out of the room," Ana explained. "I'm heading home now. I'll give you more details once I get there."

"Okay," Carlota said, hanging up.

CHAPTER

6

The Ball, the File, and the Unexpected

EVERYTHING WAS BEAUTIFUL. THE FLOWER arrangements were placed in strategic points. The band, hired for the party, would start the show right after midnight. While the guests were dancing to the sound of classical music, the waiters and waitresses would walk among them serving drinks and appetizers.

A few minutes after midnight the backyard and ballroom lights were turned off. Diane and David Thompson's guests were startled, but then they realized it was all just a preview for the band's entrance. The musicians then started the most fun show.

When the band was halfway through the fourth song, people were alarmed. They heard one of the waitresses scream when she found a dead body in the middle of the ballroom. When the music stopped, people ran inside the house to see who had fallen from the second-floor balcony.

And when they finally realized who it was, the scare was even greater.

~oOo~

Twelve Hours Earlier

Samantha was in the kitchen making lunch when she heard the doorbell ring. She put the knife on the counter and cleaned her hands on a cloth. When she opened the door, Mery was outside. They were both quiet for a long moment, just staring at each other.

"So you finally realized you were wrong and came to apologize?"

"You wish," Mery replied.

"What do you want then?"

"Unless I've done slave work for you during the talent show, I believe you owe me money. Since I remembered our deal, you owe me three hundred bucks."

"Oh," Samantha said, "you're right. Sorry. Come in. I'll pay you inside."

"No," Mery answered, "I'd rather wait out here."

~oOo~

Carla had just put her phone down when Matt entered her room. He sat on the bed and stared at his mother for a few seconds.

"Who was it?" he asked.

"It was Clark," Carla answered. "He just invited me to the mayor's party tonight."

"I didn't know that he and David were friends," Matt commented.

"They are. Thing is I don't know anyone at that party except for Clark, David, and Diane," Carla said.

"And Great-Grandma," Matt replied. "She's going to the party too."

"Is she?" Carla asked. "I spoke to her this morning, and she told me she wasn't going."

"She thought about it but then reconsidered the idea."

"Oh, this makes me more excited about going," Carla said. "Well, I gotta go, honey. I have to buy a new dress for tonight. Speaking of which, what are you doing tonight?"

"Sarah wants to go to the movies, but I don't think I want to," Matt answered. "And speaking of dresses, don't you think you already have too many?"

"One more won't make a difference."

~oOo~

Diane was sitting on the couch in the living room, turning the pages of an old photo album. David entered the room a couple of minutes later and walked toward his wife. She didn't say a thing and kept turning the pages. Once the mayor sat next to her, she stopped.

"What are you looking at?" he asked.

"I'm looking at our wedding photos," Diane replied, and David grimaced nervously. "We were so happy that day. Who could've imagined that one of us would end up cheating on the other?"

"Diane, I—"

"Don't try to tell me you're sorry again," Diane interrupted. "Because if you do that, I will be angry. More than I already am."

"What else can I do?" David yelled, standing up. "What can I say that will make you happier?"

"Watch your tone with me," she said. "You are not in the position to talk back to me."

"But I don't understand the reason for such rage!" David replied. "Yes, I had an affair, but that doesn't mean that I don't love you."

"David," Diane said, standing up and facing her husband. "David, you made a vow to God, and then you threw everything away when you decided to screw your secretary. How do you think that makes me feel?"

David didn't say a word. Diane gave a short and disbelieving laugh. She threw the photo album on the couch and glanced at her husband. David looked away and walked in the other direction, but his wife held him.

"Stay," she said. "I'll leave. I already took a long look at the past. Now it's your turn."

~oOo~

Carlota was on her front porch, sitting on a chair, admiring the beauty and peace of Crystal Street. People were friendly, gentle, and very polite. Whenever someone walked by, Carlota would wave and smile, and the neighbors would greet her the same way. Crystal Street surely was a special place.

When she was about to enter her home, Carlota heard someone calling for her. When she turned around, she saw that it was Matt. She went down the small steps of the porch and hugged the boy. Then they sat side by side on the bench and looked at their street.

"So I heard your mom is going to David's party tonight."

"Yeah, she just left to buy a dress," Matt answered.

"Who's she going with?" Carlota asked.

"Clark."

"Oh … the boyfriend?"

"Friend, not boy," Matt said and giggled. "She still introduces him as her friend, but yeah … boyfriend."

They were quiet for several minutes. A couple that was walking their dog walked by and waved at them. Matt and Carlota returned the gesture. When the neighbors walked away, Carlota and her great-grandson were quiet for a few more minutes.

"What do you think of him?"

"Who?"

"Clark," Carlota answered.

"Oh … him," Matt said. "I'm not quite sure yet. I'm still doing my research. When I'm done, I'll let you know."

"Matt," Carlota said, raising an eyebrow.

When Matt looked at his great-grandma, she had this funny smile on her face. Carlota knew he was lying.

"You know something," she finally said.

"I suspect something," Matt responded. "But I'm not sure yet."

"And what do you suspect?"

"You'll find out," he said. "Soon."

"Okay," Carlota said, standing up, "I gotta go now, dear. I have some stuff to do before the party."

"And I've gotta go get Sarah."

"Wonderful. Give her a kiss for me."

"I will."

~oOo~

When the doorbell rang, Thales went downstairs to answer the door. Ana wasn't home yet, as she was usually late whenever her office had meetings about new products. Ana worked as a publicist for a food company.

When Thales opened the door, his first impulse told him to shut it, but his politeness spoke louder than instinct. Gregory Desmond was standing outside, smiling. He greeted the boy and asked to go inside, but Thales denied the request.

"I just wanna talk to you," Gregory said.

"I'm sorry, but I don't wanna talk to you. I'm really busy right now."

"It's about the project you told me about … you know? The assignment you may need my help with?" Gregory said.

"There is no assignment, Gregory," Thales replied. "I lied."

"Why would you lie?"

"Because I know your secret."

Gregory stared at Thales for a second and started to laugh. He gave two taps on the boy's shoulder.

"You are funny, Thales. Really funny."

"I didn't make a joke," the boy replied. "We all, me and my family, are aware of your dirty laundry."

"What dirty laundry?"

"That you're no lawyer or prosecutor or whatever the hell you claim to be. We know that you are a CIA agent and that you and your wife have been lying to us this whole time. And that's why we decided to end our friendship with you guys."

"What?" Gregory asked. "That's not true. Mery was at my house this morning. We are still friends."

"No, we're not," Thales explained. "Aunt Mery was there to get her payment. After that, she left, and we're not speaking to you anymore."

"But Sam said—"

"See ... I guess we're not the only ones she's been lying to," Thales concluded, closing the door.

Gregory stood there for a long while until he decided to go back to his house. While he was walking down the street, he felt pain. His heart was broken. How could his wife, the person he loved most, do this to him after all he had done for her?

~oOo~

Adriana opened the mansion door only to find Matt standing outside. The boy smiled as the maid permitted his entrance. She followed him to the family room and waited till he sat on the couch to ask, "What are you doing here?"

"Well, I called Clark, and since he and my mother will be going to the party tonight, I asked him if I could spend the day here."

"By yourself?" Adriana said and smiled, a bit surprised. "As you know, I'll be serving the party tonight."

"I am aware of that," the boy answered. "But I won't be alone. Sarah, my girlfriend, will be here shortly."

"Oh ... so you are planning a romantic evening?"

"I guess you could call it that," Matt answered.

Adriana glanced at the boy with suspicion, but she kept her mouth shut. The maid smiled and left the room. Matt followed the lady with his eyes and looked away once she crossed the door to the kitchen.

~oOo~

It was just before six o'clock when the decorators ultimately ended the arrangements for the annual ball of Diane Thompson. Everything was in perfect harmony, except for the relatioship of the host with her husband, David. The two spent the entire day quarreling about the affair he had had with his secretary, but like all other arguments they had, David responded the only way he could by saying, "I'm sorry."

After a few more hours, Diane began to give her instructions to the members of the buffet, waiters, and Adriana, whom she had invited to help with the service since Clark and David were great friends.

"Adriana, I know this is the first time you are serving at a party in my house, but I have total trust in you."

"That's great to hear, missus," Adriana replied. "And I promise you I'll do my best so your guests have first-class service."

"That's comforting. Oh, if my husband asks for vodka, you'll bring him water."

"Won't he tell the difference?"

"Just put lemon and sugar in it … and some salt on the rim of the glass and crushed ice inside, so he thinks it's a margarita."

"But—"

"No questions. Just do what I say. And if he asks for some other kind of drink, just make something that will fool him but do not serve him alcohol."

"You're the boss."

Diane smiled and walked away, leaving Adriana and the other employees in the kitchen. When she reached the living room, Diane found David sitting on the couch, looking at their wedding album. He looked crestfallen, which moved his wife, but Diane soon composed herself and went over to him.

"Why are you looking at this?"

"Because you said it was my turn to analyze the past," David replied, staring at his wife and closing the album.

"And since when do you do what I say?"

"Many times. During my political campaigns I almost never followed the advice of my assistants and publicist. But yours—"

"Yes," Diane said and then laughed. "But I am not talking about political advice. I'm talking about life advice. You never heard me. You always did things to show people what you were capable of."

"I've always been a proud man," David replied. He got up and approached his wife. "But I often wonder if this is good or bad."

"Depends on the point of view, David. Some people say that pride is the reason for one's demise."

"So you think my pride will be the reason for my fall?" David inquired.

"Can be," Diane said, rubbing her spouse's face. "But who am I to talk? After all, I am just the naïve woman whose husband cheated on her."

Diane kissed David's lips, and he did not react. He was completely astonished at the brief conversation he had had with his wife. She walked to the yard, but before she left the room, she looked at her husband and said, "Don't be surprised, David."

"What you mean?" he asked.

"You knew a day like this could come sooner or later," Diane said and withdrew herself, leaving her husband even more distressed and much more terrified.

~oOo~

The papers were scattered all over the bed. Matt found himself kneeling beside the bed, flipping through folders and files while Sarah searched for something in the dresser drawers.

"I don't think we'll find anything here."

"But we have to find something!" Matt responded, throwing a folder on the bed and then grabbing another one that was by his side.

"Matt, if this man is as *smart* as you say, I don't think he would keep personal information in folders in his own room."

"What you mean?"

"You found cocaine in his sister's bathroom. I do not think he would be stupid enough to store things in his room. He must have hidden stuff somewhere else."

"So where do you suggest we look?"

"We could look at his parents' bedroom. What do you think?"

"That's not a bad idea," Matt said, standing up.

They left Clark's room and went to his parents' chambers. But they found nothing. And so they decided to search in Clark's sister's room. Once there, Sarah went to the closet, where she found several moldy clothes.

"Where's his sister?" Sarah asked.

"I don't know. But she doesn't come here," Matt answered.

Sarah searched her pocket and pulled out a scarf she wore on her hair from time to time. She folded the fabric and strategically placed it around her nose and mouth to prevent the passage of dust. Matt approached the girl and took off his shirt to put it around his face in order to protect himself. They took out all the clothes that were in the closet and threw everything on the bed. But to their misfortune, there was nothing else there.

"Shit," Sarah said, stamping her foot. "Let's look in another room."

"Wait. There's something there," Matt said, looking at a hole on the bottom of the wardrobe.

Matt reached out and poked his finger through the hole. Sarah stifled a cry when she thought her boyfriend's finger was caught, but instead Matt dragged the bottom of the closet to the side, revealing a false bottom.

"Oh my God," Sarah said, looking at the box under the fake bottom.

Matt picked up the box and put it on the bed. They sat on the mattress and breathed deeply before they opened the object. When they opened it, they found photos and newspaper clippings.

"What is all this?" Matt asked, picking up one of the photos.

"That is the mayor," Sarah commented. "Why would Clark keep photos of the mayor?"

"And clippings?"

"This makes no sense," Sarah said.

"Wait. There's something else here," Matt said, taking a folded paper out of the box.

The boy unfolded the paper and revealed a *plan* of the mayor's house. The drawing was done poorly, although it was full of details. Matt and Sarah analyzed the drawing very carefully until she found something that caught her attention.

"What is this?" she asked, pointing at a letter *X* that was stamped on the upper floor's home office.

"I don't know," Matt said. "There must be some kind of legend here."

Matt started to look for a legend that would reveal the meaning of the *X* stamped on the drawing. After he searched on the front, he decided to check the back of the paper, and he found the *X* drawn next to a phrase written in red, "Match point."

"Match point?" Sarah read, confused.

"This makes no sense at all," Matt answered, throwing the map inside the box. "Why would Clark have something like this?"

"This is all very strange," Sarah replied. "But I think it would be wise to put everything away and think about this in the kitchen. I'm hungry."

"All right," Matt said and smiled. "Let's go."

~oOo~

Everything was beautiful. The flower arrangements were placed at strategic points. The band that had been hired for the event would begin the show after midnight. While all the guests danced to the sound of classical music, the waiters and waitresses roamed through the various rooms of the house, serving drinks and appetizers.

A few minutes after midnight the lights of the main hall and the yard went out. The guests of Diane and David Thompson were frightened by what happened, but it was nothing. It was all prior to the entry of the band, which then started a lively and entertaining show for all gathered there.

"Diane, I must admit. This is quite a party!" Carlota said, raising her champagne glass to her friend.

"Oh, thank you, darling!" Diane laughed proudly. "And I have to say that I'm very glad that you've come."

"Well, I have my reasons. But I gotta ask you. Did you have to pick a band that loud?"

"Ah—" Diane laughed, which provoked smiles from her friends. "You know how young people are, don't you? They like noise, and David was a fan of the band, so—"

"I understand. Well, excuse me," Carlota said. "I'll be right there talking to my granddaughter."

"Oh yes, Carla's here! With the new boyfriend," Diane commented. "Clark and David are very good friends. And Clark is quite the great partyer."

"Not everyone agrees with that." Carlota smiled. She sipped her champagne and then walked away.

Carla and Clark were talking in a corner of the room when they noticed Carlota approaching. Carla ran to her grandmother and hugged her. When they let go of each other, Carla opened her mouth to say something, but

Carlota said instead, "And when are you going to introduce me to your boyfriend?"

"Oh, Grandma," Carla said and giggled, embarrassed. "Clark and I are just friends."

"Oh, please, my dear. I might be seventy years old, but I am not senile. Everyone knows that you and Clark are dating."

"Okay."

Clark reached out to Carlota, who did nothing but smile. The man quickly backed off and said, "It's a pleasure to meet you, Mrs. Carlota. Carla speaks highly of you."

"It's nice to meet you too, Clark," Carlota replied.

"And how did you come to be at this party?" the man asked while he looked nervously at Carla, who dropped a few laughs.

"Well, David, Diane and I have been friends for many years. He and my husband were practically brothers. Sure, that Jay was a little older—"

"Too much of a coincidence, isn't it, Clark?" Carla said and laughed. "Clark and the mayor are also very good friends."

"Yes," Carlota said and laughed. "Diane told me. I was quite surprised."

"It really is a small world, isn't it?" Clark asked, though he seemed distant. "Well, I am sorry, but I have to excuse myself for a moment."

"And I have to go to the restroom, my dear," Carlota said, walking away.

"But—" Carla said as she realized she was already alone.

Carla took a deep breath and sat down on the couch. She then decided to go to the backyard to honor the band that inspired all the guests.

After several minutes passed, something unexpected happened. People were alarmed suddenly. One of the waitresses gave a cry of horror when she found a body in the middle of the ballroom. The music stopped, and everyone gathered to find out who had fallen from the balcony upstairs. And when the guests saw who the person was, the shock was even greater.

Diane Thompson walked among the guests and let out a deafening scream when she saw the body of her husband lying on the floor. She kneeled next to David and stained the hem of her dress with her husband's blood. Carlota and Clark came soon after that, shocked by what had happened.

"David!" Diane yelled, shaking her husband. "Please talk to me! David!"

"Somebody call an ambulance!" Carlota shouted, stooping beside her friend. "Quickly!"

~oOo~

It was shortly after one o'clock when Clark and Carla came to the mansion. Matt and Sarah were watching TV in the living room when they heard the front door close. They both turned around to face the newcomers. Carla ran to meet her son and gave him a suffocating embrace.

"Are you okay?" Matt asked, finding his mother's reaction rather strange.

"No," Carla replied shakily.

"Oh my God, what happened?" Sarah asked as she put a hand on Carla's shoulder.

"David Thompson is dead," Carla said.

"Wait. What?" Matt asked, jumping up.

"The mayor is dead," Clark concluded with a serious tone. "Unfortunately—"

"Yes," Sarah said, raising an eyebrow, staring at the man. "Unfortunately—"

CHAPTER

7

Q&A

MATT AND SARAH WERE IN the kitchen having breakfast, while discussing the previous night's events. Clark and Carla left early that day, so the two had the house all to themselves and Adriana.

While the maid organized the rooms upstairs, Matt and Sarah took the opportunity to go into more detail about their findings and think about possible answers for their questions, since it was not practical to ask anyone about what they knew.

"According to Clark's story, he left for a while, and when he came back, David was already dead," Sarah said. "But if he had killed him, telling this story would not be right. It's too suspicious."

"Yes, but Clark doesn't know that we know the map and the box are in that fake bottom of the closet."

"You're right. But why would Clark want to assassinate the mayor? What does he gain from this?"

"I don't know," Matt said before he took a sip of juice. "But I think we can find more information here in this house."

"But where?" Sarah asked. "We scoured every room, and the only thing we found was that box."

"We could look in Adriana's bedroom," Matt replied.

"Over there? I really don't think we will find anything in her room. If Clark wanted to do everything in secret, he would not put clues in the maid's room."

"But we found the fake bottom, didn't we?" Matt asked. "What if he hid something in Adriana's room that she doesn't know about?"

"What's in my room?" Adriana inquired as she walked into the kitchen.

Matt and Sarah looked at each other in utter despair. The maid walked around the room till she reached the refrigerator. After she grabbed a bottle of water, she turned to them and said, "So ... what's in my room?"

"Umm ... we were just wondering if you have any whipped cream in your room," Sarah answered. "Because I really wanted to eat these strawberries with whipped cream."

"And what makes you think that I have whipped cream in my room?" Adriana asked, raising an eyebrow.

"I saw you taking a can from the fridge earlier," Sarah concluded.

"Very clever," Adriana said with a rogue smile. "I'll get it."

Adriana put the water bottle on the table and left the kitchen. Matt waited a few seconds before he turned to his girlfriend and said, "I'm so sorry. I froze."

"Don't worry. I am here to help you."

~oOo~

Carlota found herself lying on the couch when she heard the front door slam. Despite hearing footsteps in her direction, the matriarch of the Mackenzies did not move. After several minutes she finally heard her daughter's voice calling for her. Carlota raised her arm and waved, hoping that her daughter would see her.

"Oh ... what are you doing lying there?" Ana asked as she approached, staring at a plate on the coffee table. "Are you eating melted chocolate?"

"Death brings great changes, doesn't it?"

"Glad that you mentioned it. That was exactly what I came to talk about."

"Oh God. Please don't ask me to talk about David's death," Carlota protested, turning off the TV. "It was bad enough to witness it. I don't have to talk about it."

"Well, you're obviously very upset," Ana commented. "But talking about problems is fine. It helps to relieve the load. And I know that you and the Thompsons are very close. I can only imagine how David's passing must've struck you."

"What the fuck, Ana!" Carlota yelled. She stood up and walked around the couch. "How many times do I have to say I don't want to talk about it? I just want to be alone, eating chocolate and watching TV!"

"I know you're hurt!" Ana yelled in reply. "But you cannot turn your back on your life like this! Yes, David is dead. Was it a tragedy? Yes, but you've gotta overcome that."

Ana approached. Her mother's eyes were full of tears. The two embraced for a second, and then Ana continued, "Remember when dad died? You were devastated, but you overcame it. Sometimes life sucks, but we have to hold our heads high and move on."

"Oh my God," Carlota said, wiping away her tears. "You don't understand."

"Then help me understand. Let me help you, Mom."

"Tomorrow," Carlota replied. "I've been called to the police station to testify."

"And you're worried about that?" Ana asked, smiling. "Don't be. You had nothing to do with David's death."

"Not quite."

In that moment, Ana stepped back. Carlota sobbed again and headed for the kitchen. After a few minutes, Ana entered the room and sat down at the table. They were silent for a moment, and then Ana said, "What do you mean *not quite*?"

"No, I didn't have anything to do with David's death, but I could have had—"

"Mom, spit it out. You're scaring me. What did you do?"

~oOo~

Samantha was in the kitchen squeezing oranges for breakfast when Gregory came inside. He sat at the table and pulled out a section of the paper to read the news of the day. When he finished, he took another section and continued his slow and silent reading. Samantha noticed her husband's strange behavior and cleared her throat, but the attempt to call for her spouse's attention was a failure.

She cut another orange and cleared her throat once again. Gregory remained motionless. Samantha cleared her throat again, and finally she got the attention she wanted—almost.

"If you're having a throat problem, I suggest taking honey with lemon," he said without looking up from the newspaper. "I read a story about it in the health section."

"What's the matter with you?" Samantha asked, dropping a few oranges.

"I do not have a problem. You have a problem," Gregory replied. "Who yells before breakfast?"

"What the hell!" Samantha screamed and threw a glass against the wall. "Stop making jokes!"

"All right!" Greg retorted, clumping the paper and throwing it on the floor. "You don't want jokes anymore?"

"No, I don't!"

"Good, because I don't want any more lying," Gregory said. "Yes, I know you've been hiding things from me."

"What?" Samantha asked. "Are you going crazy, Gregory? I am not hiding things from you."

"Oh yeah? Not even the fact that the Mackenzies know I am a CIA agent? Or even that they are not our friends anymore?"

Samantha did not say a word. Gregory was way too angry. He turned around and left the kitchen. Samantha stood motionless for a few seconds until she ran after her husband.

"Gregory, come back here."

"For what? So you can lie to me even more?"

"Don't be stupid!"

"Stupid?"

"Do not forget I am not the only who's been lying in this house," Samantha said gruffly.

Gregory stepped toward her. Samantha stepped back. They both stared at each other for several minutes until he said, "Yes, I lied. But that was all so I could protect you and me. What's your excuse for hiding these things from me?"

"Umm—"

"You have no excuse!" Gregory yelled. "We had a deal, Samantha. We would lie to protect ourselves, but we would not lie to each other."

"I'm sorry," Samantha said with tears in her eyes. "I promise there will be no more secrets between us. I love you."

"I love you," Gregory replied. "And that's why it hurts me so much to tell you this."

"Tell me what?"

"I am leaving you tonight," Gregory said.

"What? No, no, no! Gregory," Samantha yelled.

"I've made up my mind, Samantha. I'm leaving this house tonight."

"But what about Jack Stappord?" she cried.

"He's dead. We saw it on the news. You'll be safe. And don't worry. Your secret is safe with me."

~oOo~

She followed the nurse to the end of the corridor. The Good Samaritan opened the door and allowed Mery Mackenzie to enter the room. When the door closed, Mery sat in a chair next to the bed. Helena was sitting on the mattress. She looked up and grinned at the sight of her friend.

"Hello, Helena," Mery said.

"Hey, it's great to see you."

"How are you?"

"Improving," Helena replied.

"Are they still giving you the pain medication?"

"No, Ana was here last week and had them suspend it," Helena explained. "It was very good of her. I was getting addicted to it. But yes, seeing you here does make me more comfortable."

"This is good to hear," Mery said with a gentle smile. "But I must apologize for not coming here before. There's so much going on."

"Incredible, isn't it?" Helena asked and laughed. "And to think that Crystal Street used to be such a peaceful place."

Mery nodded and fell silent. The two women stared at each other for several minutes. Helena stood up and walked to the barred window at the end of the room. She just stood there. She watched the scenery until she said without turning around, "You must be wondering what happened to me."

"Well," Mery answered, "yes."

"My story is quite a bit complicated, Mery."

"What you mean?"

"So much has happened in my life. It all started when I lost my job months ago."

"You lost your job?" Mery asked. "But you never told me—"

"It was not necessary. I found another one. Different from what I used to do," Helena explained, turning to her friend.

"What do you mean by *different*?"

"I began selling some products, and I earned enough money out of it. But of course, most of it would go to my supplier, but the job still paid the bills. It's funny. We think we know everyone who lives on Crystal Street, but we have no idea about what happens behind the closed doors. I had several customers."

"So this is the reason for the drugs in your dresser?" Mery asked in shock.

"Yes," Helena replied. "Although I never experimented with it until I started drinking."

"But why? How did you get to that point?"

"Well, my supplier died. So his friends in the business decided it was time to end the job. At least his. So I lost another job. And I could not bear to go through that again. I didn't want to involve you guys in all this mess."

"Oh, honey," Mery said, hugging her friend. "We're your friends, all of us. Of course we'd help you! But I hope you know that what you did was very wrong."

"Yeah, I know," Helena whimpered. "But I am very sorry for all that I've done."

"I believe you."

They hugged again. Once they were separated, Mery packed her stuff and walked to the door. Before she left, she turned to her friend and said, "I'll come back later this week."

"I'll be waiting."

~oOo~

Carlota poured the hot water from the teapot into two teacups. Ana sat at the kitchen table, shaky and completely devastated over the story her mother had told her earlier. The matriarch of the Mackenzies put tea bags in the two cups and sat in front of her daughter.

"Do the girls know about this?"

"No," Carlota answered. "For all intents and purposes, you are their sister by blood."

"I'm not talking about that! I am talking about our father! Do they know you killed our father?"

"No, they don't. Nor do they need to know."

"So why tell me?" Ana asked. "Just because I'm adopted?"

"You've know that you're adopted since the age of five," Carlota replied. "And I don't know why you're acting this way. You offered to help me."

"You murdered my father! How do you think that makes me feel?"

"I know it's a lot to digest, but I had to tell someone. I need help to go through the questioning tomorrow. If the police find out that I'm a murderer and that I had an affair with David, I could go to jail!"

"Maybe you should be arrested!" Ana retorted. "You killed a man!"

"And you expected me to do what?" Carlota cried. "Huh? Let him live so he could've killed another daughter of mine? No way! I could not save a child before you, but I would not allow him to take another one."

"You could've split!"

"That would mean he had failed. Jay Mackenzie did not fail. If I fled and divorced him after, he would have found us, and believe me, he would have killed us. I had to put an end to this story before it even happened. So that's when I decided it was time for Jay to slip and roll down the stairs."

"Is that how you did it?" Ana asked; "You pushed him?"

"Yes," Carlota confessed. "I don't know if you remember, but he had a problem with his left leg. Going up and down the stairs were his greatest difficulties. It was easy for the paramedics to believe he had slipped."

"Oh my God," Ana whimpered.

"You may think I'm a monster, but I'm not. I did what I did to protect my three daughters—you, Mery, and Cordelia. And I don't regret it, not one bit."

Carlota stood up and went around the table. She hugged her daughter and gave her a kiss on the head. Ana looked up and stared at her mother for a few seconds.

"What do you want me to do?"

"I'd appreciate it if you didn't tell anyone about this, and I want you to help me with an alibi."

~oOo~

Matt said good-bye to Sarah and waited until she entered Shirley's car to go back inside. When he closed the doors and turned around to the living room, he uttered a cry of fright when he saw Adriana standing at the top of the stairs.

"Adriana, you scared me."

"I'm sorry," the maid said. "But I needed to talk to you."

"Well, couldn't you have come here in a less silent way?"

"With that scream, I think we had plenty of noise," she said and laughed.

She walked down the stairs, passed the couch, and went into the kitchen. Matt stood there for a moment until he followed her. Once he was in the room, he found Adriana heating up some water on the stove. He sat down at the kitchen counter. Adriana glanced at him for a few seconds.

"I'm making some tea. What will you want with that?"

"Just a sandwich."

"Great call."

The two were quiet for several minutes until Adriana finished preparing the snacks. She poured Matt some tea and handed him a plate with his sandwich. Then she pulled up a bench and sat in front of Matt.

"So what do you think of the sandwich?"

"It's great," Matt answered. "But I'm curious. What were you so eager to talk to me about?"

"Oh … that."

Adriana was silent for a moment. She took a bite of her sandwich and a sip of tea. After she swallowed, she wiped her mouth with a napkin and said calmly and slowly, "What were you and Sarah talking about this morning?"

"Nothing important. Why?" Matt responded, playing dumb.

"Ah, Matt. I may be the maid, but that does not mean I'm stupid," Adriana said and smiled. "I know you two were talking about Clark."

"Then why ask?"

"So you *were* talking about him."

"How can you be so sure?" Matt asked with a rogue smile.

"You confirmed it."

"Did I? I must say I don't remember doing so."

Matt wiped his mouth and stood up. He took his dishes to the sink and started to wash them when Adriana approached. She held his hand and said, "You don't have to do this."

"I want to," Matt replied. "Gimme your wares too."

"Matt," Adriana said and then started giving her dishes to him. "Why were you talking about Clark?"

"Why are you so curious about that?" Matt asked. "The last time we spoke about him, you said you wouldn't help me. So as you already know what I'm up to, I see no reason to ask questions."

"You should be careful, Matt," Adriana said.

Matt dried his hands, turned off the tap, and walked away. When he reached the kitchen door, he turned to her and said, "I am being careful, Adriana, and considering that you will not tell on me, I think I'm out of danger for now."

~oOo~

Metal detector, inspection, hallway—that was the way Carlota Mackenzie walked to reach the waiting room of the Greendale Police Station. When she entered the room, she found Diane Thompson sitting in the corner, her eyes swollen and red. Carlota approached her friend.

"Hello, darling."

"Carlota?" Diane asked, looking up at her friend. "Oh, my gosh."

The first lady stood up and hugged her friend. After the hug they both sat down. Carlota removed her sunglasses and put them in her purse. Diane pulled out a handkerchief and wiped her tears.

"I cannot believe you're here. How did you know I was going to be questioned today?"

"Well, I didn't. I had an idea, but I'm here because they also called me to testify."

"What?" Diane inquired, surprised. "But why?"

"I don't know."

"I thought the police had interrogated all the guests at the party."

"Yes, they asked me questions, but they still called me."

At that moment, the doors of the waiting room opened, and an unexpected person entered the room. Clark wore a gray suit, which suited him nicely, with a blue tie and a black shirt. He approached the women, greeted them, and took the chair next to Diane.

"Diane, I can only imagine the pain you must be feeling," Clark said. "I am so sorry for your loss. David was a great friend."

"Thank you," Diane replied before she blew her nose.

"So, Clark—" Carlota began, raising an eyebrow, "you were also called for questioning?"

"Ah, yes … and frankly I don't know why. They questioned me at the party."

"They've questioned everyone at the party," Diane replied.

"Does that mean we are suspects?"

"Most likely," Carlota concluded.

The three fell silent. They sat for a few more minutes until the detective left the questioning room and walked toward them.

"Hello, I am Detective Davis, and I will conduct the hearing today. Mr. Abromheit, come with me, please."

Clark nodded and stood up. The men walked away, leaving the women behind. After a few minutes of silence,

Carlota stiffened and poked Diane's shoulder. The widow turned to her friend, who asked, "What do you think of him?"

"Clark? I think he's an amazing person," Diane said in response. "Why?"

"I think there's something odd about him. Problem is that I don't know what."

"You suspect people too much, Carlota," Diane said. "You should stop this, really."

~oOo~

Diane entered the interrogation room and crossed paths with Clark on the way in. The two parted ways, and the widow took her friend's seat inside. Detective Davis walked in a couple of minutes later and closed the door. He was holding a cup of coffee and took the seat in front of the first lady.

"Ma'am, I am sorry for your loss."

"Thank you," Diane said, staring at the iron table in front of her.

"I know this is somewhat unpleasant, bringing you here today."

"Not only unpleasant but inconvenient, Detective," Diane replied. "My husband is dead. I should be at my house, grieving and planning the wake and the funeral, but no. I'm being interrogated. My question is why."

"I'm sorry, Mrs. Thompson, but I'll be asking the questions around here," the detective said. "Where were you at the time your husband died?"

"I was in the backyard … with my guests. I heard the scream and went inside. When I got there, David was dead."

"You seem quite relaxed for having lost a husband in such a brutal way."

"Believe me, Detective—I'm devastated. I've cried a lot," Diane explained. "I was crying until minutes before coming here, but sometimes in a marriage there are times when you feel relieved."

"So you feel relieved by the death of your husband?"

"Kind of."

Davis took a sip of his coffee and cleared his throat. He wiped his mouth with a handkerchief he pulled from his jacket pocket and said slowly, "Mrs. Thompson, I quizzed all your guests at the party. Many of them said that you and your husband were going through a rough time. Is that accurate?"

"With all due respect, Detective, every marriage has problems," Diane said. "But if you must know, yes, we were going through a hard time."

"Some of your guests mentioned an affair," Davis replied. "But nothing concrete."

Diane looked at the detective without saying a single word. The man got up and left the room. He returned a few minutes later with a box of tissues and a cup of coffee. He handed the objects to the widow. Diane took the objects and put them on the table. She took two sips of coffee, grabbed a tissue, and wiped her mouth. Then she pulled out another tissue and held on to it.

"Yes, my husband was cheating on me."

She used the tissue she was holding to wipe some tears that started to run down her face. The detective straightened himself on his chair and said, "Did you kill your husband?"

"No, I did not."

"Mrs. Thompson, some of your friends told me at the party that you were spreading the news that you had a surprise planned for David."

"Yes, I did," Diane said, dropping the tissue. "But don't think that the surprise was his assassination. I would announce our divorce to everyone and say that he actually cheated on me."

"But what would you get out of this?"

"He would run again next year for his second term," Diane explained. "An affair and a divorce would shatter his career and would make his numbers go downhill. Would I be humiliated? Yes, but seeing him fall would be comfort enough."

~oOo~

When Diane left the interrogation room, Carlota was called to go inside. She occupied the chair her friend had sat in before her and waited for the detective to go back inside. Davis sat at the table and gave a forced grin, but Carlota did not care.

"Let's cut to the chase, Mrs. Mackenzie."

"Oh yeah, I'm not here to small talk," Carlota answered. "Let me tell you what I know. David Thompson and I have been friends for over thirty years. We've been a little estranged, but we came back to being friends. He was cheating on his wife, and I was very angry. But I didn't kill him."

"And you expect me to believe that?" Davis said and smiled.

"Yes," Carlota replied. "Detective, I am a seventy-year-old woman. Do you really think I could fight David? He may be in his fifties, but everyone knows that the mayor was a great fighter."

"Let's say you didn't kill him," Davis asked. "And you said that you were angry because he betrayed his wife. Did you do something about it?"

"David invited me to dinner," the matriarch of the Mackenzies said. "I accepted. And there we talked about it. But it all ended in a weird way when his mistress appeared and made a scandal."

"And what did you do?"

"I did what I had to do! I forced David to take the right attitude. And then he ended the affair right there. The other day I found out she had revealed everything to Diane."

"What are you suggesting?"

"I'm saying that you might have two suspects on your hands," Carlota answered. "Clark and the lover."

"Why Clark?"

"Well, he's dating my granddaughter. I don't like him, and I think he's hiding something. And I'd never met him before, and then I found out he's great friends with the mayor. Is he the killer? I don't know, but he could be."

"So your guess is Clark or Michelle?" Davis asked.

"Yes. And if you were good at your job, you would know that I'm telling you the truth. I did not stutter or hesitate, and I answered all your questions with complete sentences. I believe those are signs of the truth."

"You clearly do your homework, don't you?" the detective asked.

"No, Detective, I am simply an honest person, unlike some of those who sat in front of you, meaning Clark."

"What do you mean?"

"Find out. Isn't that your job?"

"Where were you during the murder?" Davis asked.

Carlota stood up and walked toward the door. She turned around and said, "I was on the phone with my daughter, Ana. If you doubt me, call her."

"And what if you're lying about all those things?"

"Then I guess you'll have reasons to arrest me," Carlota replied. "Have a nice day, Detective."

She opened the door and walked out. Davis smiled and exited the room minutes later.

Chapter
8

Father and Son

CARLA CAME HOME LATE AT night. She and Clark were at the movies, and after that, they went to a restaurant. When she got home, she hung her purse on the hanger and left her car keys on the counter next to the door. Carla went to the kitchen so she could get a glass of water. Once she was in the room, she read the headline of the newspaper that was lying on the table: "Vice Mayor takes office after the bizarre death of David Thompson."

Carla poured the water in a glass and went upstairs. When she was halfway down the hall on the upper floor, she heard a noise and turned around. Matt was looking at her from his bedroom.

"Matt, you scared me. I thought you were asleep."

"No," the boy answered, "I can't sleep."

"Oh … come with me."

Matt nodded and followed his mother to the master suite. When they got there, he sat on the bed and waited till his mother changed her clothes in the bathroom. Carla came out of the bedroom with her pink robe on and sat next to her son.

"So why can't you sleep?"

"I have a lot on my mind."

"What?" Carla said and laughed. "Matt, you're seventeen. How can you have so much stuff in your head that you can't sleep?"

"Well, my life is not like the lives of kids my age," he answered. "But I'm okay with that."

"What's been bothering you? You can be honest with me."

"Okay, I know it's hard, but I have to ask you this."

"Matt," Carla said, "you're scaring me."

"I want you to stay away from Clark," Matt finally said.

"What?" Carla exclaimed, surprised. "Why would you ask me such a thing?"

"He is not who you think! I'm trying to protect you!"

"Protect me from what, Matt? Clark is a nice guy, and he makes me happy!" Carla snapped, standing up.

"Have you ever stopped to think that he could've killed David?" Matt asked. "He was called in for questioning today!"

"So what? Grandma was called in as well! Do you think she's a killer?"

"That's different! I have reasons to believe that Clark is the culprit! And I think it would be wise to take him to the police."

Carla turned her back and rubbed her hair. Matt stared at his mother for several seconds without saying a single word. Carla turned to her son and said, "I don't want to hear anything else about this! Do you understand me?"

"For the love of God, Mother, open your eyes! You're dating a murderer!"

"He's not a murderer!" Carla yelled. "Stop saying that!"

"Fine," Matt concluded. "But I will take him to the police."

"Matt, if you take him to the police—"

"Don't worry. I won't report him right away. I have to collect more evidence first."

~oOo~

The next day Carlota was having lunch with her friend Diane Thompson. The widow was still very upset with the whole situation. At every instant, reporters and journalists were making up articles and talking about Diane's feelings and what she thought about the vice mayor occupying the office.

The women arrived at the French bistro together. They went to the receptionist's counter, and Diane gave her name. The woman guided the clients to their table. Carlota and her friend sat in front of each other and asked for a bottle of wine.

"So—" Carlota started. "How are you?"

"I'm fine," Diane said. "But I'm still quite depressed."

"I know how you feel. When Jay died, I was in the same situation."

"But your husband wasn't murdered."

Carlota gulped and smiled sheepishly before she said, "Yes, but his death was as bizarre as David's."

At that moment, the waiter came and poured wine for the ladies. They then decided it was time to order their meals. The boy wrote everything down on a pad of paper and walked away. A few minutes later he returned with a basket of bread and a plate with olive oil. When he left, Carlota grabbed a piece of bread and dipped it in the olive oil. Once she ate it, she took a sip of wine. Diane did the same thing.

"Can I ask you a question?"

"Yes," Carlota answered, "you can ask me anything."

"What did you tell Detective Davis yesterday in the police station?"

"Does it matter?"

"Yes," Diane said and laughed. "See, Carlota, it's not that I think you're the one to blame, but I wouldn't be happy if you had lied."

"Wait. So you think I killed your husband?" Carlota asked, outraged.

"No, but I'd like to hear what you told the detective. After all, it was all very strange at the party."

"What was?"

"The way you came. When they found David, you came a few minutes later. Where were you?"

"I was taking a piss!" Carlota said louder than she expected, which caused everyone to look at her. "I cannot believe you actually think I'm capable of killing your husband!"

The waiter returned and placed a plate of escargot on the table. Carlota picked up her cutlery and took the little snail out of its shell. She dipped it in a sauce of herbs and ate it.

"I'm sorry, but I really need to find the culprit."

"Diane, I know you're desperate to know who the killer is, but have you thought that maybe he could've killed himself?"

"What?" Diane asked. "No, David would not be capable of that."

"How can you be so sure?" Carlota asked. "What if he did kill himself? Maybe he was unhappy and felt sorry for the harm he had caused you. Between us, he loved you a lot, but he cheated. Maybe he was sorry, and he thought that the only way to fix things was by taking his own life."

"I never stopped to see that side, but I don't think it's possible. David was too proud. He wouldn't take his own life."

"We don't know what goes on in people's minds, especially of those we think we know more."

"Maybe you're right," Diane said. "But you have yet to tell me what you told the detective yesterday."

"I told him the truth, Diane. I told him I did not kill your husband."

"That's it? And he believed you?"

"Much more than you believe me," Carlota replied.

"Carlota—"

"Don't Carlota me. I will not be Carlota'd! I cannot believe that you, my best friend, don't trust me!"

"I do … and I don't."

"Then stay with your doubts, Diane!" Carlota replied. "Now here's a question for you. What makes you more innocent than me?"

"I do not understand."

"How can we make sure that you didn't kill your husband? After all, you're the cuckold, which gives you more reason to kill him than anyone! Enjoy your lunch!"

Carlota threw a hundred-dollar bill on the table and left. Diane stared at her plate with a discredited look. Had she lost her husband and best friend consecutively?

~oOo~

Sarah collapsed on the bed and climbed over to Matt. They were both sweaty and panting. She grabbed the blanket and covered herself. Sarah ran a hand over Matt's chest and continued down to his thigh, but Matt held her hand.

"I can't do it again."

"Oh, really?" Sarah said and laughed.

"Oh, really?" Matt repeated. "We've done it three times this afternoon."

"But you're not always like this—"

"It must be because I'm angry."

"Angry?"

"Yes, Mom and I had a fight last night," Matt said.

"Because of Clark?" Sarah asked. "She won't leave him, will she?"

"She won't—meaning that I have to find more evidence."

"Yeah, but for that you'll have to go to his house."

"Problem is that after last night my visits to his house are over," Matt replied.

Sarah and Matt kissed. She uncovered herself and hugged him. Suddenly she opened her eyes and smiled.

"Oh, I guess someone's excited."

"Maybe."

"I'll handle this," Sarah said and winked.

She crawled over and started to kiss Matt's belly. He closed his eyes and relaxed. A few minutes later he sat on the bed and pulled Sarah down to him. Sarah bit her lip and sat on Matt's lap. She kissed him.

"Maybe," Sarah moaned, "we could go to his house when he and your mother go out."

"You know," Matt said as he pressed Sarah's hips and kissed her neck, "that's not a bad idea."

"I know it's not," Sarah said between moans. "But we should finish this first."

~oOo~

One thing you should know is that since the last time Mery visited Helena, the latter was in a rehab center. Cordelia and Mery decided to split the costs of the center so that Helena could make a quick recovery. When she came out of the hospital, she was transferred to the Greendale Rehab Center.

On a certain Tuesday morning, Cordelia and Mery decided to go and visit Helena together. When they got there, the doctors and nurses rushed from one side to another. Everyone seemed very frightened about something that had happened there. The sisters approached the information desk. The nurse responsible hastily talked on the phone. Mery waved to announce her arrival, but the woman merely raised a finger and kept on with her conversation.

After a few minutes, the woman hung up the phone, and Cordelia approached the counter.

"Hi, we would like to visit our friend Helena Trevers."

"Well, I don't know if you can tell, but we have a situation on our hands."

"It's hard not to notice," Mery said. "But we will not be in your way. We would just like to see our friend."

"As it turns out, the situation we're having is because of your friend," the clerk replied.

"What do you mean?" Cordelia asked.

"Miss Mackenzie!" a man said and approached. "I am Dr. Parker, Helena's psychiatrist."

"Oh, of course. We met the other day."

"Hi, the name's Mery. I'm Cordelia's sister. Could you tell us what's going on here?"

"Umm … it seems that Helena has escaped."

"What? What do you mean escaped?" Mery yelled. "What kind of rehab center is this?"

"What do you mean by *seems*? You mean you've lost her?" Cordelia asked.

"Please, I ask you to calm down," Parker said. "She's still in the building, but we cannot locate her."

"This is absurd!" Mery said. "What are we paying you for?"

"We've gotta find her," Cordelia replied. "C'mon, Mery."

Mery and Cordelia ran in the opposite direction of the psychiatrist. They both looked through several rooms along the corridor, but there was no sign of Helena. The sisters got to the staircase leading to the lower floor. Cordelia went ahead. The windows along the steps revealed the leisure garden for the patients, and there they saw Helena.

"Oh my God, Cordelia!" Mery yelled, pointing out the window. "There's Helena!"

"She's jumping the fence!" Cordelia screamed. "Help! Somebody, help!

At that moment two nurses and Helena's doctor arrived at the stairs. Mery pointed out the window, revealing Helena about to jump the wall surrounding the center. The psychiatrist and his nurses ran down the stairs. Helena's friends followed.

Once they reached the garden, they walked among the patients. Mery and Cordelia reached the fence. Helena was already on the other side, and then she ran across the street.

"Helena, no! Don't do this!" Cordelia yelled.

Helena turned around. She stopped and stared at her friend. Cordelia waved and told her friend to walk back to the rehab center, but the woman did not move.

"Watch out!" Mery shouted. "Helena, watch out! The car!"

When Helena realized where she was, the car hit her. She rolled over the vehicle and fell on the street. The driver accelerated and disappeared. Mery and Cordelia did not move. They were in complete shock from what they had just witnessed.

The sisters and some medics at the rehabilitation center left the building and went up the street. People who were passing by started to gather around to watch the scene. Mery and Cordelia crouched beside Helena, who was covered in bruises and had blood dripping from her forehead and the corner of her mouth.

"Helena, please wake up!" Cordelia said, sobbing.

"Don't do this," Mery said, rubbing her friend's forehead. "Stay here."

~oOo~

Carla was having a cup of coffee in the kitchen when the doorbell rang. She put the cup on the table and went to answer the door. When she opened it, she faced someone extremely unexpected.

"Hello, Carla," Robert said with a grin.

"What are you doing here? I told you at the restaurant that I didn't wanna talk to you!"

"I know, but we need to talk."

"After eighteen years without hearing from you, I think we have nothing to talk about!" Carla backed off and tried to close the door, but Robert stopped her. "Robert, let go of the door, or I will call the police!"

"You will not!" he said.

"Do not test me!"

"Please, let me in. I promise to behave."

Carla rolled her eyes and opened the door and allowed her ex-husband to enter. They went to the kitchen, where Carla offered Robert a cup of coffee. He nodded, and she poured. Carla sat at the table with him but did not say a word.

"I see you remodeled a bit."

"I wouldn't keep the same decoration, not after what you did. Too many bad memories."

Robert smiled and sipped his coffee. They were silent for several minutes. Carla could not even look at him without feeling the urge to spit in his face. After half an hour of torturing silence, she finally said, "What do you want?"

"I came to apologize … for everything that I've done. All my choices were wrong. Abandoning you like that was the worst thing I could've done."

"What?" Carla asked, perplexed. "And it took you eighteen years to realize that? Unbelievable."

"Yeah, I know it's absurd, but it's true! I am so sorry!"

"Robert, the judge had to grant me a divorce because you simply vanished. You should not be asking for forgiveness. You should be thanking me! I didn't ask for the police to find you so I could get a pension. Because of me, you escaped going to jail."

"I know," Robert said, crestfallen. "But now I'm back, and I hope I can be a part of Matt's life."

"And you expect him to accept you with open arms?" Carla asked and laughed. "If yes, you're the same idiot I married."

At that moment they heard the front door close. Carla sat up straight on her chair and waited. Robert lowered his head and started to play with his cup. Suddenly Matt appeared at the kitchen door. He stared at his mother and the man for a second.

"Who's that?"

"I think you might wanna sit," Carla said, pushing a chair toward her son.

After Matt sat down, Carla waited a few seconds so she could talk, but it was Robert who instead said, "Hey, Matt—"

"Do I know you?" the boy asked suspiciously.

"No," Carla said, "but he *knows* you."

"All right. Who's he?"

"I'm your father, Matt."

~oOo~

Ana and Thales were eating cookies in the kitchen when the phone rang. Ana stood up and answered the call. Suddenly Thales heard a noise and turned to his mother. Ana knocked the phone on the floor, and the portable shattered.

"What happened?" Thales asked, standing up.

"Helena is dead."

"What? Oh my God!"

"We have to tell the others."

Thales and his mother ran outside. They parted ways and rushed to their relatives' houses. When Thales told Carlota about Helena, she almost fainted in shock. They went inside, where the boy poured some water for his grandmother. Once she was finished drinking, Carlota turned to her grandson and asked, "How did this happen?"

"I don't know. Mom didn't tell me."

"We should go to Carla's house. Ana must be there."

Thales and Carlota went to Carla's house, and when they got there, Ana was standing outside. She had her ear pressed against the wall to listen to the screams that were coming from inside the house.

"What's going on?" Thales asked as he approached his mother.

"Shut up!" she said. "I'm trying to find out."

"Who's that voice? They're not alone in there," Carlota commented.

At that moment, Matt opened the door. Ana stepped back and almost fell on her back. The boy stopped, astonished, realizing his family had been snooping. Carlota climbed the porch steps and grabbed her great-grandson's shoulders.

"What happened?"

"You don't wanna know."

Robert and Carla suddenly appeared behind the boy. Ana and Carlota stifled a scream and turned pale, as if they had seen a ghost. Matt walked away from his great-grandmother as she approached Carla and Robert. The man offered a sheepish smile and said, "Hello, Carlota, how are you?"

"What the fuck are you doing here?" Carlota asked.

"I came to see my son."

"You don't have children here, Robert!" Carla yelled, pushing the man.

"That's not true!"

"Oh, but it is!" Matt yelled, turning around to face his father. "You did not look for me all this time, and now you want a relationship?"

"How many times do I have to apologize?" Robert asked.

"Your excuses, *Father*, are worth nothing to me."

"I think you can see that you're not welcome here," Carla said. "Get off my property."

"Or we'll call the police," Carlota concluded.

Robert nodded and walked away. As he descended the porch steps, Ana and Thales approached their relatives. Carlota waited a few more seconds until she said, "Helena's dead."

"Wait. What?" Carla asked.

"How?" Matt exclaimed in shock.

"She tried to run away from the rehab center," Ana explained. "When she jumped the fence, she was hit by a car, and the person drove off."

"Oh my God. Who told you this?"

"Aunt Cordelia called," Thales explained. "She and Aunt Mery are at the center."

"Let's go there."

"I can take you," Robert said, approaching.

Matt came down the porch steps and approached his father. They stared at each other for a few minutes until the boy said with determination, "At some point I must've given you the impression that I wanna be in the space that you're in, but believe me, it's not true."

"Robert, please go away. Don't make this harder than it already is."

~oOo~

When they all arrived at the rehab center, the members of the Mackenzie family met Cordelia and Mery at the reception desk. The women led their relatives to the upper floor, where they'd have a meeting with Helena's psychiatrist, Dr. Parker.

Matt and Thales decided to stay outside the room so that they didn't meddle in the situation. The others entered the psychiatrist's office and Carlota locked the door so they wouldn't be disturbed.

The boys sat on the corridor floor next to a pillar and remained silent for several minutes until Matt asked his cousin, "Is there any possibility, however small, that you've already followed my advice?"

"What advice?" Thales asked, though he already knew the answer.

"The advice I gave you the day before the talent show. About telling your mother about what you told me?"

"Oh, that. Well, not yet."

"Thales!"

"But wait," Thales said. "Let me finish. I didn't tell her because she's been going through a lot of stress lately. She's been having problems with a coworker, and I don't wanna bother her even more."

"I understand what you mean," Matt replied. "But there are things we cannot postpone. And I have business I have to attend to. I cannot keep your secrets forever. I have my own to worry about."

"You have secrets?" Thales asked.

"Not exactly. I am trying to figure out someone's secrets."

"Matt, what are you talking about?"

"I don't know. I mean … it's weird. But that person is hiding something, and I could be putting my life in danger by trying to figure it all out. But it's all for a good cause. I'll save my mother."

"Matt, oh my God."

At that moment, Matt stifled a scream of rage when he saw Robert walking down the corridor toward him. The boys stood and started walking in the opposite direction. Matt's father began to follow them down the hallway until he finally reached him.

"Matt, stop!"

"What do you want?"

"I wanna talk to you!" Robert said. "You are my son."

"No, I am not your son!" Matt replied. "You abandoned me, so do not expect me to love you! I don't want a relationship with you or your money or your love!"

"Don't say that."

"Believe it! I lived for seventeen years without those things from you, and I turned out just fine. And it's not because you're here now that things have to change. I do not love you!"

"Fine," Robert said, crestfallen. "I'm leaving ... for now."

"Don't!" Matt said. "I don't want you to come back. I want you out of my life just like you've been these past years."

"Let me buy you and your mother dinner," Robert suggested. "Please, that's my last request. I'll come to pick you up Friday at eight o'clock. Be ready. If you don't wanna go, I'll leave and never come back. We can talk at dinner, and if you don't want anything from me, I'll understand."

"Fine!"

Robert smiled and walked away. The boys stared at the man, who disappeared around the bend of the corridor. Matt leaned against the wall and slowly sat down on the floor. Thales sat next to his cousin and asked, "Are you going to the dinner?"

"No," Matt answered. "If I don't go, he'll be out of my life a lot faster."

"And do you think this is the right choice?"

"What you mean?"

"Matt," Thales explained, "I have no father. My father died when I was ten."

"I know what you're doing, so stop. It won't work," Matt replied.

"No! Now it's my turn to give you some advice!" Thales said firmly. "Go and have dinner with your father."

"He left me, Thales. Why would I give him a chance?"

"He abandoned you? Yes, he did. But now he's here begging for your forgiveness. Give him a second chance!"

"And why would I do that?"

"Because you have no idea how bad it is to grow up without a father."

"Yes, I do." Matt said. "I grew up without mine!"

"No, you don't! I had my father until I was ten. Your father was gone, but he's still alive. You know what I'd give for my father to have simply abandoned me?" Thales asked with tears in his eyes. "I'd give anything for him to still be alive, whether he liked me or not. So take my advice. Go out with your dad … and enjoy yourself. Because one day the worst could happen, and you'll regret everything."

"Do you regret anything?"

"Oh yes," Thales answered, "I regret a lot of stuff."

CHAPTER
9

As expected, the whole neighborhood attended Helena's wake and burial. Since she had no family, the Mackenzies decided to take on the expenses. The Mass in Helena's honor was one of the most beautiful ones they had seen, even better than Erick Woodard's, the deceased mailman.

After the burial, some of the residents of Crystal Street joined Carlota and her family at her house for a small brunch. When the neighbors left, the Mackenzies were the only ones left to help Carlota with the mess.

When they finished, the Mackenzies gathered in the living room for one last cup of hot chocolate with cookies. As they ate and drank their hot beverages, the family talked about Helena and remembered the great moments they had spent alongside her. The conversation was interrupted by Cordelia saying, "So what do we do now?"

"What you mean?" Ana asked.

"I mean, Helena ran away from the rehab center under their watch. If they had taken care of her, she'd still be alive."

"Grandma's right," Matt said. "This cannot stay like this."

"And what do you suggest?" Carlota asked. "There's not much to be done. Helena had no family, so they can't solve anything."

"Yes, she had no family, but she had us," Carla said. "I think we can take action."

"If you're talking about suing the rehab center," Thales said, "I totally agree. We were paying for everything. Helena was our responsibility."

"Perfect!" Mery said, clapping her hands. "I agree. Let's sue them!"

"Stop with this nonsense!" Carlota yelled, beating her thighs. "We will not win this case!"

"It doesn't matter!" Cordelia replied. "We can at least try. Besides, the public humiliation will be enough to end the rehab center's reputation."

"But we're not Helena's family! There's no way we can start this process."

"Yes, there is," Thales explained. "Our money was being invested in Helena's treatment. Their neglect toward Helena is our concern. Yes, we have reason enough to open this process."

"Indeed," Matt said. "There's a chance."

"It's settled then!" Mery said and celebrated. "Cordelia and I will visit the rehab center later this week so that we can announce the process. We'll take care of everything we need."

~oOo~

Samantha was preparing some tea when she heard the doorbell ring. She turned off the fire and went to answer the door. On the outside there was Gregory, sweaty and shaky. Samantha invited him in, and the two went to the kitchen. When they sat down at the table, Samantha turned to her husband and asked, "What happened? You look terrible."

"Oh, Samantha ... a terrible thing," Gregory replied.

"Look. If you're trying to win me back, you don't need much effort. I love you, Greg."

"It's not that."

"Oh," Samantha said, a little saddened. "What then?"

Gregory was silent for a few minutes. He lowered his head and started to cry. Samantha stood up and walked around the table. She knelt beside her husband and took his hands in hers.

"Tell me what happened. I didn't mean to be rude."

Gregory stood up and went to the sink. He picked up a glass from the cupboard and poured himself some water. Samantha stood up and leaned against the counter. When he finished his water, Gregory cleared his throat and said, "What I'll tell you can be pretty shocking, but I need you to help me."

"Greg, you're scaring me."

"I—" he stammered.

"For God's sake, spit it out!" Samantha said firmly.

"I ran over Helena," Gregory said.

"Oh my God."

Samantha covered her mouth with her hands and said nothing. Gregory collapsed in a chair at the table and waited until his wife composed herself. Samantha came around the counter and grabbed a container on the cabinet. She dumped two spoonfuls of sugar in a glass and filled it with water and drank it all.

When she finished drinking, Samantha washed the glasses and the spoon and put everything back in its place. Then she put the container back on the cabinet and approached her husband. Gregory lifted his head to face her and opened his mouth to say something, but Samantha hit him with a slap that made him fall from his chair.

"It was an accident. I swear!"

"Helena was hit by a car that sped away!" Samantha yelled. "How could you do this?"

"I got distracted when my phone fell on the floor, and when I saw she was in the middle of the street, there was no time to swerve."

"Do you have any idea how serious this is? And you are CIA!"

"Why do you think I ran?" Gregory asked. "This could destroy my career. I'd lose my badge and spend years in jail!"

"I have to tell the police, Greg. I'm sorry."

"Samantha, don't do it. Please," the man begged. "I can't be arrested!"

"Why should I help you?" Samantha asked. "You left me. I have no more reasons to protect you."

"Oh, I think you have," Gregory said, standing up. "I thought you'd help without pressure, but I've just realized this is my only way out."

"You're gonna blackmail me? You have nothing against me that won't incriminate yourself."

"No? But what if I tell the police that you used to sell drugs with Jack Stappord? Or that you killed a cop?"

Samantha gulped and stayed quiet for a few seconds. Gregory approached his wife and said, "Everybody has their little dirty laundry. Problem is you and I can only rely on ourselves."

"We gotta get rid of your car," Samantha replied. "If someone on the street recognizes it, we can say that it was no longer in our hands."

"But how did I get here?" Gregory asked.

"By taxi. You will now put the car in the garage. At dawn we'll get rid of it."

"The car's already in the garage."

"Great. I'll start dinner. You can rest, and later we can put our plan into action."

~oOo~

Carla and Matt arrived at the restaurant around eight o'clock. When they entered, Clark was waiting at a table. The two approached and greeted the man. A few minutes later Clark stood and went to the restroom. That's when Carla grabbed her son's arm and said, "I hope you can behave tonight!"

"Mother," Matt said with a cynical tone, "I may not like him, but that doesn't mean I'll be rude."

"Don't talk to me like that!" Carla whispered angrily.

"If you don't know this, I am still mad at you," Matt replied. "This man is not trustworthy, and I am trying to show you this. But you'd rather not listen to me."

"It's not quite like that. I just think you should end this—" Carla said. "Nobody thinks the same way you do."

"Is that really what you think?" Matt said and laughed. "Then Mom, you should study the facts. I am not the only one who thinks you should end your relationship with Clark."

At that moment Clark returned from the restroom and sat down again. He put his napkin on his lap and stared at his companions for a few minutes until he asked, "Were you two fighting?"

"What? No," Carla said and laughed nervously. "We were just talking. Matt?"

"Yes," Matt answered. "So Clark, what do you suggest I order?"

"Well, there's a salmon with a parmesan risotto. It's really good," Clark replied. "I usually have that, but today I'm having steak."

"Awesome. I'll have the salmon," Matt said with a smile.

Minutes later the waiter came and took their orders. When the dishes came, everyone at the table fell silent and tasted the wonderful flavor of the restaurant's food. After dinner Clark ordered dessert to share with Carla since Matt refused the offer.

When the couple finished their dessert, Matt went to the restroom, and Clark asked for the check. When Matt came back, he saw the waiter handing the check to his mother. Carla took three hundred dollars out of her purse and handed it to the waiter. The young man smiled and walked away.

"So, shall we go?" Matt asked as he approached his party.

"Sure," Carla said.

The three left the restaurant, and Carla walked away to get the car. Clark and Matt were all alone, waiting for her to come back. They were silent for several minutes until the boy finally asked, "So … three hundred dollars for one dinner. You should not spend that kind of money, Clark. Saving—that's how people remain rich."

"I didn't pay for dinner," Clark replied, "so I think I'm safe."

"If you didn't pay, who did?"

"Your mother."

"But I thought you invited us for dinner."

"That's right. I did."

"Then why did she pay?" Matt retorted. "I believe the boyfriend is supposed to pay. I mean, I'm not asking for you to pay for my food, but you could at least pay for yours and hers."

Clark turned to Matt and asked with dissatisfaction, "What are you doing?"

"Nothing. I'm just showing you how ugly what you do is. In most couples the guy pays for dinner, not the woman. If she pays, then she should pay for hers only. Sarah and I are an example."

"There are couples that do what your mother and I do," Clark replied. "Like you said … *most couples*."

"I said most, Clark, because I don't want your situation to get worse. The only couple that does what you're doing is you and mom. But don't worry. I am sure next time you'll open your wallet."

"What makes you think that I'll change? And who do you think you are to tell me how to drive this relationship with your mother?"

"I am the son of the woman you're dating, so I think I'm entitled to some opinion about your relationship. Besides, you don't wanna mess with me."

"And why is that?" Clark said and laughed contemptuously.

"Because, my friend, I can be just as devious as you are, and that … is something you wouldn't be able to handle."

~oOo~

The next day Carlota decided to stay home and watch some old classic movies from when she was younger. She prepared a few sweets and went to the supermarket to get a few cans of soda. When she came back home, Carlota encountered an unexpected visitor. She parked the car in the driveway, grabbed her shopping bag, and went to the porch, where she met Detective Davis.

Carlota approached the man and greeted him. Detective Davis grinned and took the bag out of her hand. She thanked him and unlocked the door. She invited the detective into her house, and they went to the kitchen, where Carlota put her groceries in the fridge.

"You want to eat or drink something?"

"No, thanks," the detective replied.

"May I ask what you are doing here?"

"I came to talk to you."

"I hope this has nothing to do with David's death," Carlota said.

"Unfortunately, it has," Davis answered. "I'd like to know one thing."

"Oh—"

"The other day I interrogated Michelle, the deceased's lover," Davis explained. "She told me that you and David went out to dinner one time."

"I told you about this dinner the other day. He wanted to thank me for taking care of his wife when she was shot."

"But Michelle felt like you and David had an affair. Is that true?"

Carlota paused and swallowed. She never expected anyone else to know about her affair with David. The detective approached and asked, "Is that true?"

"It's complicated."

"So you did have an affair with him?"

"I never said that," Carlota answered. "My relationship with David was more than a mere affair. It was comfort."

"Comfort?" Davis asked.

"Yes. My husband had died, and David was the only person who gave me comfort. And while we talked, some feelings popped up, and we got into this relationship."

"Why didn't you tell me this?"

"I don't see how this is relevant to the case. David and I had something years ago. When he died, we were nothing but friends."

"Carlota, I really want to believe you, but you omitted information."

"Detective Davis, I'm not asking you to believe me. Just do your job. But in the end you'll realize I am innocent."

"I know you say that you're innocent, but how can I trust you?"

"You can't," Carlota replied with a smile.

~oOo~

Cordelia and Mery were sitting on the porch when they saw Carla approaching. They waved and called for her to join them. Cordelia made room for her daughter so that she could sit next to her. Mery analyzed her niece and noticed that something was wrong. Carla looked dejected and upset about something.

"What happened?"

"What you mean?" Carla asked, trying to avoid the subject.

"You seem sad. What's going on?"

"Mery is right," Cordelia said. "C'mon, honey. Talk to us."

Carla closed her eyes and breathed deeply. The women stared at her for several minutes until she said, "I had lunch with Clark today."

"And he broke up with you!" Mery said with enthusiasm.

"No!" Carla snapped.

"Oh—" the aunt said, trying to hide her disappointment. "Then what happened?"

"At lunch I asked Clark about his relatives," Carla explained. "You know … mother, father, siblings."

"And what did he say?" Cordelia asked.

"He started to cry. And then he told me the most shocking story. And I regretted my question as soon as he began!"

"What did he tell you?" Mery asked curiously.

"His father had serious mental issues and killed Susan, Clark's sister," Carla told them. "His mother died a few days later from a heart attack."

"What about his father?"

"He killed himself."

"God," Cordelia said in shock. "So many tragedies in one family."

"But you shouldn't feel bad about it," Mery said. "You didn't know anything. It was an honest question with no intention of hurting anyone."

"I know, but Clark is such a good man for me, and to see him hurt makes me sad," Carla explained.

Mery breathed slowly and checked her wristwatch. She jumped out of her seat, looked at Cordelia, and said, "Sis, we gotta go! It's time for our meeting."

"Oh yeah!" Cordelia said, standing up and looking at Carla. "And you, my daughter, don't beat yourself up because of this. I'm sure he's not angry at you."

~oOo~

"Don't say that," Detective Davis said as he walked around the counter. "You lied, but you still gave me a reason to trust you."

"Why are you so eager to trust me?" Carlota asked, walking away from the detective.

She opened the fridge and got herself a can of Coke. She opened her drink and sipped twice. The detective approached her and touched her shoulders. Carlota widened her eyes and tried to pull herself away, but the man was too strong for her.

"I wanna trust you because of all people I've interrogated in my entire career, you're the one who's been honest with me, except for that one omission of yours."

"Well, I'm flattered," Carlota said and then laughed, a little embarrassed. "But you might wanna let me go. My arm is hurting."

"I'm sorry," he said, loosening his grip.

Carlota sipped her drink one more time and glanced suspiciously at the detective. The man was sweating, and he had a strange look on his face. His eyes were fixed on her. Carlota turned around and walked slowly toward the sink that was filled with water and some dirty dishes.

"I think you should go. If you have no more questions for me, that is."

"Why do you want me to go? Do you have any commitments today?"

"I do ... with myself," Carlota answered. "I'm gonna watch some classic movie from my teenage days."

The detective approached, raising an eyebrow. Carlota put her hand surreptitiously into the sink. She started looking for something she could use to defend herself. It was clear that Detective Davis was not a sane person.

"You know, Carlota, you fascinate me by the minute. Even in a delicate situation like this, you still find some time to have fun."

"I fascinate you?"

"Yes, you are an amazing, beautiful, and intelligent woman."

The detective approached her a little bit more and pressed his thighs against Carlota's butt. She closed her eyes, trembling. The man put his hands on her waist and glided up. When he was about to touch her breasts, Carlota turned around and stepped away from the detective.

"What are you doing?" she asked and stared at him.

"I'm doing what we both want."

"Detective Davis, I'm old enough to be your grandmother."

"It doesn't matter. Age is just a number. And you have the spirit of a young woman. And your looks—" Davis said, biting his lower lip.

"Thanks, but I really think you should go."

"Really?" he asked. "I think I could stay a little longer."

Davis approached Carlota, and she leaned over the counter. She opened a drawer and felt around for an object between the cutleries. When David leaned against her, Carlota struck him with a knife. The detective cried out and walked away.

"You shouldn't have done that."

"Get out of my house … right now!" Carlota said firmly.

"I am a cop. I could have you arrested for that!" Davis said angrily.

"I don't care who you are. I just want you to leave."

He stepped forward, but then he stopped when Carlota pointed the knife at him.

"I swear to God if you ever touch me again, I'm gonna fucking kill you."

Detective Davis gave Carlota one last look and covered his wound with his hand. When he left the kitchen, Carlota heard the front door closing. She dropped the knife on the floor and sat on a chair, wiping her forehead sweat with one of her hands.

~oOo~

Mery and Cordelia didn't have to wait long at the rehab center. The psychiatrist, who was also the supervisor of the site, called them in less than ten minutes of their arrival. He guided the women to his office and asked his secretary to fetch them some coffee. When the young lady returned, she served the doctor and his guests and left the room.

When the girl left, Dr. Walter Price, the supervisor, put on his glasses and brushed his mustache with his fingers. Mery opened her purse and handed him a file. The man picked it up and removed the small elastic that held the document together.

"What is this?" he asked, flipping the papers.

"Those documents address a recent event that took place here at your rehab center," Cordelia explained. "I think you know what we mean."

"You're referring to Helena Trevers, aren't you?"

"Exactly," Mery said, nodding and adding some sugar to her coffee. "Not only to her but also to your negligence with a patient."

"Mrs. Mackenzie," the doctor said, "we are not negligent."

"Oh, aren't you?" Cordelia said and laughed. "I'm sorry. So please, Doctor, find another word that describes you better. Because if memory serves me right, one of your psychiatrists, Dr. Parker, prescribed Helena some pain medication."

"And in case you didn't know, Helena was an addict, not to medicine but to many other things—drugs, alcohol. And as you might know, pain medications are known for turning people into addicts," Mery concluded. "It wasn't until my sister Ana met with Dr. Parker that he suspended the use of those medications. No wonder Helena had a relapse."

Dr. Price closed the folder and gave it back to Mery, and then he stood up with his coffee cup in his hand. The psychiatrist walked to the barred window of his office and stared at the gardens for several minutes. Then he turned to the women and said, "Dr. Parker is a professional that's more than competent."

"Then you must be more than incompetent," Mery shouted. "If Dr. Parker knew about Helena's condition, he shouldn't have done what he did!"

"He must've had a reason to prescribe the medication."

"That doesn't justify anything!" Cordelia commented. "He made a serious mistake, and you as a supervisor and a much more experienced man should confirm this! We spent money on this institution, Dr. Price."

"This is not an institution," the supervisor interrupted. "This is a rehab center."

"Institution or not," Mery started, "you should take responsibility for the consequences. We're paying you. Helena's death is on your hands."

"Pay attention," the doctor said as he returned to his chair. "Dr. Parker has been with us for years now, and he had never lost a patient before, so there is nothing I can do. Besides, Dr. Parker and I have a theory."

"I can't wait to hear it!" Cordelia said and laughed. "I bet it'll be inspiring."

"The best way to end an addiction is by acquiring another addiction."

"So you and the brilliant Dr. Parker thought together and decided to overdose your patients?" Mery asked, perplexed. "Are you mentally ill? Dr. Price, I never expected to hear this from you. I bet the newspapers and magazines that give you support will be pretty shocked when they hear all of this."

"Mery, I think we're done here," Cordelia said. "Just wait, Dr. Price. We're gonna meet again."

"What are you gonna do?" he asked and laughed, "Sue me?"

"You bet your ass we will," Mery said. "And now that we've recorded our entire meeting, I believe we have a little more chance of winning."

"Have a great day, Doctor. See you in court."

Cordelia and her sister stood up and left the office, leaving the psychiatrist in complete disbelief. When the sisters left the supervisor's room, they went to the reception desk. The nurse responsible for the reception area hung up the phone when she saw the women approaching.

"Can I help you?"

"Yes," Mery answered, "we came to collect the belongings of Helena Trevers. She died a few days ago."

"Oh, sure," the nurse said. "I'll be right back with her box."

The nurse walked away and went through a door that led to a dark hallway. While they were waiting for the nurse to come back, another nurse approached. She poked Cordelia's shoulder and asked, "Excuse me. Could you do me a favor?"

"Sure, hon."

"Tell Abigail that Nurse Diva needs her help in Susan Abromheit's room. Here is her record."

"Okay," Cordelia said, grabbing the file.

When Nurse Diva walked away, Cordelia put the record on the table and turned to her sister. When she opened her mouth to speak, Mery yelled, "Susan Abromheit!"

"Do you know her?"

"No, but oh my God!"

Mery grabbed Susan's record and pulled out the first page. She and Cordelia read the paper from beginning to end and from end to beginning. Once they were finished, they looked at each other, aghast.

"Is this who I think it is?"

"Cordelia, oh my God," Mery said, terrified.

~oOo~

When Samantha came into the living room, she encountered Gregory looking out the window at the starry sky. He was curled up in his favorite chair. Samantha approached her husband and knelt at his feet. Gregory looked at his wife and slowly smiled, somewhat crestfallen.

"It's time."

"Already?" Gregory asked, closing his eyes tightly. "Can't we wait a little bit longer?"

"No!" Samantha snapped. "We have to do it now. It's our only chance. Let's go!"

Gregory stood up slowly and followed his wife into the kitchen. They walked through the door that led into the garage. Samantha entered Gregory's car as he entered hers. A few moments later they left the garage and drove off from Crystal Street.

Minutes later the couple was on the highway. That was the perfect spot for Samantha's plan. Gregory parked the car on the side road and watched his wife push his car over the hill. Suddenly the man heard his phone ring.

"Samantha?"

"It's done."

"Yeah, now let's get the fuck outta there!" Gregory said before he hung up.

Seconds later Gregory was startled when Samantha knocked on the car's window. She entered the vehicle and locked the doors. Greg turned to his wife and said, "What now?"

"We leave," Samantha answered firmly. "Let's go."

Gregory accelerated and left the place. Samantha looked out the window for a moment and realized that was not the way to her house. She turned to her husband and asked, "Where are we going?"

"To my apartment. From there you can drive to your house, and then we can move on with our separate lives. The lawyer will call you in a few days."

"What?"

"You heard me," he answered.

"You called a lawyer? When?" Samantha asked in shock.

"The day I left you," Gregory said. "Samantha, this is for the best, and you know it."

"No! I will not sign off on a divorce! It's not what I want!"

"But that's what I want, Sam!" Gregory replied after he stopped the car.

Samantha looked out the window and saw the place her husband had settled in after the separation. It wasn't a big building, but it was very luxurious. The couple was silent for a few seconds until Gregory unbuckled his seat belt and opened the car door. When he stepped outside, Samantha said between sobs, "I thought that after all we went through, we could be together."

"Well, you can only blame yourself for this."

"Gregory, I helped you escape from prison for homicide," Samantha commented. "The only thing I could hope for after that was for you to come back home."

"Samantha, it wasn't murder," Gregory replied.

"Then what was it?" Samantha yelled. "You ran her over, and you fled. And now, thanks to me, no one will know."

"We got together for one last time," he concluded. "But our marriage is over."

"We united to hide another crime," Samantha said and then laughed ironically. "That's perfect. Who was I kidding anyway? A marriage that revolves around crimes and secrets could never work."

"We were fooling ourselves."

~oOo~

Matt was lying on the couch and watching TV when he heard the doorbell ring. He stood up and walked to the door. When he opened the door, he encountered his aunt Mery standing outside. The aunt smiled and entered her nephew's house. They hugged for a moment and then went to the living room.

Mery sat on the couch, and Matt sat on the chair on the other side. They were silent for a few minutes until the boy asked, "Do you want something? Juice? Water? Soda?"

"No, thanks," Mery answered. "I just wanna talk to you."

"Oh … did I do something wrong?"

"No!" Mery said and laughed. "Of course not."

Mery fell silent. The boy put his legs on the chair and waited for his aunt to resume speaking. Mery straightened on the couch, cleared her throat, and continued calmly and slowly. "Today your mother came to talk to me and your grandmother. She was very upset about a conversation she had with Clark at lunchtime."

"Really?" Matt asked. "I hope it wasn't because of the conversation I had with him the other day."

"It has nothing to do with you."

Matt raised an eyebrow and lowered his legs. Mery straightened her neck and stretched a little more forward and rested her elbows on her thighs. She took a deep breath and continued, "She asked Clark about his family—mother, father, siblings."

"And what did he say?"

"Well, he said that his father suffered from mental problems and killed Susan, Clark's sister."

"Oh my God!" Matt said, covering his mouth.

"Soon after, Clark's father committed suicide. His mother died soon thereafter," Mery said. "Your mother was upset because Clark was really shaken up by the conversation."

"Well, it wasn't her fault. She didn't know," Matt commented. "But I still don't understand why you're telling me this."

"After that I went to the rehab center with Cordelia to talk about the process. When we were waiting for Helena's things, a nurse gave Cordelia a record of a patient so she could hand it to another nurse. Just one simple favor. That's when we noticed something very strange ... and terrifying."

"Aunt Mery, you're making me nervous," Matt said, a little disconcerted. "What did you see in the record?"

"The patient in question," Mery continued, "was Susan Abromheit."

"What?" Matt asked. "But Clark said his sister was dead!"

"That's the sinister part. According to the record, Clark was the one that put his sister there."

"Oh my God, but why would he do that?"

"I don't know," Mery replied. "But you gotta find out, Matt. I think Carla is in danger, and so are you."

"I'll find out everything I can as soon as possible."

"And go to the police. Something tells me that Clark should not be loose. He has a secret, and I believe it's a pretty bad one."

CHAPTER
10

As the time passes, everyone strives to forget certain things. Some carry the things they witness for the rest of their lives. There are also those things people laugh about in the future. However, in the middle of all happenings, good or bad, there are those decisions and actions that sometimes haunt people forever. No matter how hard people try to forget them, they will always be there. *The past will always come back to haunt us.*

~oOo~

On Thursday morning Adriana was sitting in the lounge, reading the newspaper that was delivered earlier that day. She flipped through the news, and she didn't even realize when Clark entered the room. The man cleared his throat and gained his maid's attention. Adriana closed the paper and put it on the table. She stood up and walked to the kitchen.

Once she was in the room, she grabbed a jug of juice and poured the drink in the glass, which she then handed to Clark as he sat at the table. She got two eggs from the fridge and some cheese and ham and started to prepare an omelet. Once she was done, she put the food on a plate and gave it to her boss.

While Clark ate his breakfast, Adriana prepared herself a sandwich and a cup of coffee. When she finished, she sat on the stool next to the kitchen counter. At that moment, Clark finished eating and took his dirty dishes to the sink. And then something happened. The man started to wash the dishes. Adriana was astonished. She approached her boss and closed the tap.

"What are you doing?"

"Washing the dishes," Clark replied casually.

"But that's my job. You don't even know how to work the dishwasher."

"We need to talk," Clark said. "But first I'd like to know what you were reading in the police section of the newspaper."

"I was reading about the investigation of the mayor's death," Adriana explained. "It seems that the case will be closed since the police can't find anything that leads to the killer. But Detective Davis will continue working on the case ... off the books most likely."

"Is that good or bad?"

"I guess a little bit of both. But let's forget about it. What do you want to talk to me about?"

Clark smiled nervously. He dried his hands and leaned against the counter and faced Adriana. She crossed her arms and raised an eyebrow. They were silent for a moment. Then Clark said, "What I have to tell you is a bit serious."

"Oh—"

"You know those bricks I keep under the sink, don't you?"

"Yes," Adriana answered. "What about them?"

"As it happens, when I bought them, I didn't pay for the delivery," Clark explained. "And yesterday he charged me the money, so I had to pay for it."

"But your dealer is dead. How come you had to pay?"

Clark smiled and left the kitchen. Adriana rolled her eyes and ran after her boss who was almost at the mansion's door. The maid stopped in the middle of the living room and shouted, "Clark! Don't you dare leave this house without explaining this story to me! Jack Stappord died. Why the fuck did you have to pay for the drugs?"

"He didn't die, Adriana," Clark said, approaching his maid. "The body the police found contained Jack's DNA because he faked his own death."

"Why'd he do that?"

"I don't know, but he showed up here yesterday."

"How come I didn't see him?"

"You were at the grocery store," Clark answered. "Jack Stappord came here, took the money, and left."

"Shocking, but okay," Adriana said. "What I don't understand is where I come in … in all of this."

Clark suddenly started sweating. He trembled and sat down on the couch. Adriana raised an eyebrow and stepped closer to her boss. She touched his forehead. He was cold and pale. She pulled the newspaper off the coffee table and sat in front of her boss.

"What's going on?"

"I—" Clark stammered and then stood up. "I have no money to pay you anymore."

"What?"

"Jack Stappord took everything I had!" Clark explained. "I have nothing left!"

"But what about your bank accounts? Savings?" Adriana asked, pacing from side to side. "Because this clearly is an emergency!"

"He cleaned out all my accounts."

Adriana turned around to face him very slowly. He was shaky and sweaty, and that all got worse when he saw the look on his maid's face. It seemed like she was going to explode with rage. Her eyes were red and filled with tears, and her lips were pale and dry. Adriana walked slowly toward her boss, who stepped back.

"How could you let this happen?" she yelled.

"I had to pay him!" Clark said. "I have twenty packs of cocaine upstairs!"

"Twenty packs? You have way more than that! You have cocaine that you bought three years ago! You don't sniff that shit anymore, Clark! You just buy it out of spite!"

"I know, but I can't control myself!"

"We had a deal, Clark. And what the fuck are we gonna do now?" Adriana asked. "I'm sure you don't want your secret to be revealed."

"You're gonna tell on me?"

"I don't know. Will I have to?"

"What do you want?" he asked.

"Let me continue living here in one of the rooms upstairs. Since I'm no longer your maid, there's no need for me to stay down here."

"Fine … but I hope you find another job."

"I will. I'm not like you. I'm not happy to sit around the house all day."

~oOo~

Samantha was watching TV while drinking coffee and eating a sandwich she had prepared earlier. She was watching *House of Cards* with Kevin Spacey when the doorbell suddenly rang.

She stood up and walked to the door. When she turned the knob and opened the door a little, her first impulse was to close it and call the police, but Jack Stappord pushed her inside and entered the house.

With the strength of the push, Samantha fell to the floor. Jack closed the front door and locked it. He walked slowly toward Samantha and smiled. She crawled back to the stairs and sat on a step. She looked at him for a second and said, "You're supposed to be dead! I saw the news!"

"Interesting, isn't it?" he said and laughed. "And smart too. I faked my own death, and no one knows about it, except for you and an old client. But none of you will say a thing."

"What do you want?" Samantha asked, standing up, leaning on the railing.

"Oh, Sam, I missed your naïve way. I want you … dead. But I won't kill you now. I want Gregory first."

Samantha approached Jack Stappord with a smile on her face. They stared at each other in silence for several minutes until she said with conviction, "Too bad. Gregory left me. We're getting a divorce. So you might as well kill me now because it'll make no difference."

"You must be pretty dumb, Samantha. Do you really think Gregory would miss an opportunity to come to your rescue?" Jack Stappord said and laughed. "If he finds out you're in danger, he'll come in the blink of an eye."

"What makes you think that?"

"He loves you."

"Not anymore," Samantha replied.

"Do you really think that a CIA agent would risk his entire career to save one woman? That's called love, my dear."

"How can you tell what it is? You're unable to love anyone!"

"Oh, but I do know how to love! I loved you. I still love you, but you deserve to die. You broke my heart. You almost told the police about me, but you didn't because you realized it wouldn't benefit you. So, Samantha, will I have to threaten you, or are you gonna call Gregory?"

"I won't call him," Samantha said with determination. "This is between you and me."

Stappord rolled his eyes and put his hand on his back. As he pulled his arm back, he pointed his gun at Samantha's head. She stifled a cry of horror and started to shake. The dealer took two steps forward and said in her ear, "Pick up your goddamn phone, or I'll blow your fucking head off. And then I'll kill Gregory."

"Why don't you just do it? You're gonna kill him anyway."

"Oh, no!" Jack laughed and stepped away. "This is the brilliant part! I won't kill Gregory. I'm going to kill you in front of him! Thus, he'll feel what it's like to have someone you love taken away from you."

"What?" Samantha asked.

"He took you away from me. And now I'm gonna take you away from him."

~oOo~

Mery had just left her house to pick up her mail. She opened the door of the mailbox and checked the letters to see if everything was correct since Erick Woodard's replacement used to mix all the mail. And to her frustration, Mery found a letter addressed to Samantha among her things.

"Shit!"

The woman closed the mailbox and headed to her neighbor's house. Once she arrived, she looked at Samantha's car parked in the driveway. Mery knocked on the door but got no response. After she knocked on the door and rang the doorbell several times, she decided to go inside, but the door was locked. Mery lifted the welcome carpet and got a copy of the key Samantha kept there. She unlocked the door and walked in.

"Samantha? This is Mery. I know you're here. I can see your car."

Mery got no response. She closed the door and kept walking. She checked the living room, but the place was deserted.

"Samantha, don't play deaf with me. I have one of your letters. Come out. I don't wanna be here anymore. What the hell, Samantha? Where are you?"

"Mery, get out!" Samantha's voice echoed through the room. "Get out now!"

"Are you okay?"

"Mery, run!" Samantha yelled. "Don't stay here. Run!"

Mery felt Samantha was in trouble, but she decided to obey. She left the letter on the counter and turned around. When she opened the door, she came across a man pointing a gun to her head. Mery stifled a cry and retreated into the house. Jack Stappord entered the house and locked the door once again.

"How did you get in here?"

"I know where Samantha keeps the spare key," Mery said, her hands up.

At that moment, Samantha appeared in the hall. Her appearance was disheveled, and a sleeve on her shirt had been torn at the shoulder. Her pants were dirty with a white powder that Mery recognized as wheat. And on her forehead Samantha had a cut, and blood trickled down the side of her head.

"Mery," Samantha gasped. "Jack, let her go!"

"Yes, let me go!" Mery said. "I did nothing wrong. I just brought the letter that was delivered to me by mistake."

"Shut up!" Jack said, pointing the gun at them. "She stays. If anyone comes in this house, they'll stay. Mery, isn't it? Go outside, grab the spare key, and if you try to run, I'll shoot your ass."

Mery nodded and walked slowly outside. She grabbed the key and went back inside the house. She locked the door and handed it to her captor, who thanked her and put the key in his pocket. Samantha walked toward Mery and held her hand. Despite being angry with her neighbor, Mery did not resist the act of affection.

"What happened to you?"

"He attacked me," Samantha answered with tears in her eyes.

"By the way, who are you?"

"Oh, where are my manners?" Jack said before he bowed. "I am Jack Stappord!"

"Wait. What? You died! I saw it on the news!"

"He faked his own death," Samantha explained. "And now he's back."

"But what does he want with you?" Mery asked, confused.

"Everything will be explained when Samantha decides to call her husband."

"Where's Gregory?"

"He left me," Samantha answered.

"Honey, I am so sorry," Mery said.

Samantha smiled, and they both hugged. And it was in that moment that Mery forgot all about her friend lying and forgave her. Jack rolled his eyes and said aloud, startling his hostages, "How lovely! Now … who will make the call?"

"I will," Mery said finally. "I'll talk to Gregory."

"I like your friend, Samantha!" Jack said and laughed. "Perhaps I shall kill her first so she won't suffer when I euthanize you."

"What should I say to him?" Mery asked without reacting to Jack's comment.

"Tell him that Samantha needs him because I'm here. And say that if he calls the police, I'm gonna kill her, so he must come alone!"

Mery nodded and went to the kitchen. Once there, she saw the mess. There were broken dishes, water leaking from the sink, an open jar of wheat, and a bloodstain on the floor. Mery breathed deeply and began to sweat. Her nerves were bustling with the whole situation. She took her phone out of her pocket and dialed Gregory's number. A few seconds later he answered the call.

"Mery?"

"Hello, Gregory. Thank God you picked it up!"

"Did something happen?"

"Greg, Jack Stappord is here!" Mery said.

"What?" Gregory exclaimed.

"He's here. Samantha and I are hostages. He told me to tell you to come alone because if you call the police, he's gonna kill us both."

"I'm on my way!"

"Gregory, tell my family. They can call the police."

Mery hung up and put the phone in her pocket. When she returned to the living room, she found Samantha sitting on the couch. Jack stared out the window. Mery sat next to her friend and cleared her throat to get her captor's attention. Jack turned around and smiled.

"You have a beautiful street. Did you call him?"

"Yes, he's on his way, and he won't call the police," Mery said.

"Gimme your phone," Jack said.

"What? I won't give you my phone!"

"Gimme your fucking phone! Do you wanna die?" Jack yelled, standing up.

Mery closed her eyes and gave Jack her phone. The man unlocked the phone and checked Mery's last phone calls. He smiled and gave her the cellular back. She grinned and put it away.

Jack sat on the chair that faced the couch and pointed his gun at the ladies. They were silent for several minutes until Samantha said, "I'm hungry."

"Funny that you mentioned that, because so am I," Jack said and smiled. "You don't have to prepare anything. We'll order some Chinese. Mery, do you want something?"

"No, thank you."

"You want yakisoba with vegetables?" Samantha asked.

"You know me too well!" Jack laughed.

She rolled her eyes and walked to the phone so she could order the food. Meanwhile, Jack and Mery remained seated, facing each other.

~oOo~

Gregory stopped the car in front of Carla's house. He left the vehicle and ran to his neighbor's porch. He rang the doorbell quickly and repeatedly. A few seconds later Carla appeared breathless at the door.

"Gregory, what are you doing here?"

"We need to talk."

Carla was a little perplexed by the way Gregory entered her house. She followed him to the kitchen and poured herself some water as she gave him a can of Coca-Cola.

"What happened, Gregory? You look nervous."

"Carla, you need to call the police."

"What?" Carla said and then laughed, confused. "Call the police?"

"Yes, Samantha and Mery are hostages," Gregory said.

Carla dropped her glass on the floor, and it shattered into pieces. She was completely shocked by the news.

"Oh my God! What do you mean?"

"No time to explain. Call the police and tell them to go to my house!"

Gregory finished his sentence and ran toward the door. Carla ran after her neighbor. She reached him when he was leaving her garden.

"Gregory, where are you going?"

"I'm gonna save them."

Gregory gave Carla one last look and walked away. The woman watched her neighbor until she heard footsteps behind her. As she turned around, Matt was standing right behind her. The boy looked disheveled. He wore nothing but shorts. He was probably asleep minutes before.

"What's going on?"

"I need you to do me a favor."

"What?"

"Call your father and cancel dinner," Carla replied. "We will not be able to go."

"Why?" Matt asked.

"Aunt Mery is in trouble."

"What kind of trouble?"

"No time to explain! Just do what I say and meet me at Ana's!"

Matt nodded and ran into the house. Carla picked up her phone and called the police as she ran to Ana's house.

~oOo~

Gregory grabbed the doorknob, but the door was locked. He rang the bell and waited a few seconds until Jack opened the door. They stared at each other, and Jack grinned.

"Hello, Gregory."

"Jack."

"Come on in."

When Gregory walked in, Jack closed and locked the door once again. The men went to the living room, where they met Samantha and Mery. Samantha stood up and ran toward her husband. He held her in a warm embrace. Jack entered the room a few seconds later and pointed his gun at his hostages.

"Now that we're all together with an outsider," he said, looking at Mery, "we can begin our little party."

"Jack, leave Mery out of this," Gregory said. "She has nothing to do with it."

"Now she does … and shut the fuck up! You'll only speak when I tell you to."

"Look, this is a free country. Everyone has the right of speech. So we can talk whenever we want," Mery said. "I'm not a part of this drama of yours, so I can't even understand what's going on here. You should be dead, but you're not. You wanna kill them, but you also wanna kill me, an outsider. This is all very confusing."

"You will understand in just a second," Jack replied.

~oOo~

The members of the Mackenzie family—all except Mery—were gathered in Ana's living room. Carla told them about the recent situation that Mery, Samantha, and Gregory found themselves in. All of them were shocked by what they heard, but they all sought to take the appropriate action.

"We cannot just break into the house," Carlota said. "We could get hurt."

"Yeah, but we cannot let Mery die in there!" Ana protested.

"Mom already called the police," Matt said. "And Gregory is CIA."

"Matt is right," Thales observed. "With the police on their way and with Gregory inside, I believe they're safe."

"Maybe, but we gotta keep monitoring this situation," Carlota said, standing up. "If the police don't arrive, we must keep calling."

At that moment the front door opened. And they were all surprised when they saw Robert standing before them in the living room. Matt got up and went to meet his father. Robert tried to hug his son, but the boy walked away. They went to the kitchen so they could talk privately.

"What are you doing here?"

"I was worried. When you told me that Mery was in trouble, I thought I could help," Robert explained. "Speaking of which, where is she?"

"She's a hostage at the house on the end of the street. But don't worry. We've called the police. Samantha's husband is CIA, and he's in the there too, so they'll probably be fine."

Matt was silent for a few seconds just like his father. They stared at each other until the boy said, "But I might need your help."

"Really?" Robert asked in excitement. "What for?"

"I still need a confirmation. If I find out that what I know is true, I'll call you, Robert."

"Robert?"

"It's your name, isn't it?"

"Yes, but I thought you were calling me Dad," Robert said, crestfallen.

"It will take a while to get used to this idea," Matt replied as he walked back to the living room.

~oOo~

Jack was sitting on the chair, throwing his gun from one hand to another. His hostages looked at him with anger, fury, and discomfort. He stood up and said slowly, "You all seem bored."

"We are!" Mery replied. "How sweet of you to notice."

"Ah, Mery, I love your sense of humor … and your intelligence," Jack said and laughed. "But you have some temper."

"Really? I think it's because I'm a hostage in a story that does not concern me. I still don't know what it is!"

Jack Stapford nodded and glanced at Gregory. The agent stood up and put his hand on his back. The captor pointed his gun at Samantha's head and said, "Put your gun on the floor and kick it to me … or I blow her head off."

Gregory did exactly what Jack told him to do. Jack smiled and got his rival's gun. He sat on his chair and looked at Gregory for a few seconds.

"I think we should tell the story."

"Maybe—"

"Wonderful!" Jack said and laughed. "I'll start!"

"Oh, stop bouncing around and tell the story!" Samantha roared. "Let's get this over with."

"Several years ago, twenty to be exact, I met Samantha. She lived here. We started dating, and I presented my work to her. Trafficking. Despite the scare, Samantha did not leave me and started working with me. One beautiful day, maybe not so beautiful, a CIA agent appeared."

"And Samantha fell in love," Mery said, staring at her friend.

"That's right, Mery!" Jack said and applauded. "She fell in love! Of course I could not let her stay with him because I loved her. Still do. So I killed one of our customers—a cop! But the blame fell on her. Nothing could lead them to me, only her."

"That's when I decided to ask Samantha to marry me," Gregory explained. "She hesitated, but she accepted. We got married in secret, and then we fled. My coworkers knew what I had done, but they helped me cover it up. My department believes that I was on a mission to catch Jack."

"And so I came back," Samantha said. "We spent all those years hiding. And then I decided it was time to come back home. And then the news about Jack's death came on television. We were so relieved. But now he's here."

"It's an interesting story, isn't it?" Jack mocked. "A love triangle. I spent all those years trying to track them until I finally found them. I hired a friend to get rid of them, but he shot the mayor's wife instead."

"Oh my God!" Mery exclaimed. "That was you?"

"Yeah. So I killed my partner and faked my death. I asked my henchmen to fire everyone who worked for me, including one of your neighbors, Helena Trevers."

"What?" Mery and Samantha asked in unison.

"So that's why she became an alcoholic! Helena's death is your fault!" Mery retorted.

Samantha and Gregory stared at each other quietly. Jack Stappord stood up but said nothing. Mery ran a hand through her hair and asked, "And how did you get here?"

"I went to a former client's house," Jack explained. "He owed me some money, so I went there to get it. I bought this gun and a few bullets and came here. I might as well give Clark a bit of his money back. After all, he helped me finish my revenge."

"Clark?" Mery asked. "What Clark?"

"My client, Clark Abromheit." Jack laughed. "Who knew, right?"

"Oh my God!" Mery said, looking at Samantha. "He's dating Carla."

"Greg, you gotta do something."

"So what are you planning now?" Mery asked. "You will simply kill the three of us?"

"Oh no," Jack said and laughed. "I'll kill Samantha. So Gregory will finally feel just like how I felt when he took her from me. And I will kill you. Just for fun!"

"You're crazy!" Samantha said, standing up. "I did the right thing by leaving you! I don't even know how I let myself fall for you. I'm glad that Gregory appeared because he made me stop looking at your shitty face every day, you monster!"

"Wow," Jack said. "I never expected to hear this from you, Samantha. But you just made things a lot easier."

Jack pointed his gun at her and fired. Mery uttered a cry of horror as Samantha fell on the couch. The blood trickled down her stomach and stained the couch and her clothes. Mery put Samantha's head in her lap and started to cry.

"Sam, please open your eyes. Don't die. It'll be fine."

"You bastard!" Gregory yelled as he pulled a gun that he had hidden on his leg. "Didn't see that one coming, did you?"

"I actually did." Jack laughed, shooting Gregory.

The shot grazed his arm, and he dropped the gun. Gregory ran in the opposite direction as Jack fired twice more. Mery removed her cardigan and covered Samantha's wound in an effort to stop the bleeding.

~oOo~

The members of the Mackenzie family were still in the living room when they heard the shots. They all rose to their feet and dialed 911. Then they ran outside where the other residents of Crystal Street were standing.

"Someone call the police!" a woman who couldn't stop crying shouted.

"We already called them!" Carlota replied.

Another shot was fired. The bullet went through the window and hit the crying woman. The other residents of Crystal Street panicked, and chaos descended. People where running, pushing, screaming, and hiding. The Mackenzies ran to Carla's house, the nearest place, and took refuge in the living room. Ana pulled out her phone and called an ambulance to rescue her wounded neighbor. After a few minutes the shooting stopped, but no one dared to leave their houses.

~oOo~

Jack Stappord stood with his gun in hand. Mery was bloody, trying to stop Samantha's bleeding as she grew paler. But Gregory was nowhere to be seen.

"Please you gotta let me take her to a hospital!" Mery said, sobbing. "She will die!"

"That's my goal!" Jack said and laughed. "Leave her there. She's already dead. And you'll be next!"

Mery didn't attach much importance to what Jack had told her. Unlike many, Mery Mackenzie was never afraid to die. She believed that if she died it was her time. Because of that, a lot of people considered her to be a cold person, which made her quite angry.

While she was trying to help her friend, Mery started to observe Jack's movements and came to a simple conclusion. He was extremely calculating, and he was a perfectionist. He made all his movements after a lot of thinking, unlike Gregory, who improvised most of the time.

Is that a flaw or a virtue? Mery thought to herself when Jack left the living room and went into the kitchen, his gun always facing forward. *Maybe a bit of both. Perfectionism is good. Nothing goes wrong. But calculating is also good. It helps with achieving perfection. However, these characteristics makes us slow to take certain actions. That's it!*

Eureka! Mery reached a solution. She stood up very slowly and rested Samantha's head on a cushion. She walked to the kitchen and grabbed a knife that she quickly hid in her pocket the moment that Jack Stappord returned to the room.

"What the fuck are you doing here?" Jack asked, pointing his gun at her. "Go back to the living room! Now!"

"I just came to get some paper towels," Mery said, sobbing as she grabbed the paper roll.

"You've got your paper towels. Now get outta here, you bitch!"

Mery nodded and went to the living room. She pulled the knife out of her pocket and hid it behind the pillow Samantha was lying on. Jack came back to the living room minutes later. He was all sweaty and red.

"Gregory, come out, come out, wherever you are! Come and face me, CIA! *Mano a mano!*"

"You know, Jack," Mery said. "I think you'll lose."

"No," Jack said and laughed. "You want me to lose, but I'll kill you all."

"I did some thinking," Mery continued. "You plan your actions in advance. And then you calculate and make them perfect. But this may be your downfall."

"What do you mean?"

"I mean, you can easily beat Gregory if you want. But he improvises, and that's what gives him the advantage. You are slow, Jack. If you wanna beat your enemy, you gotta think like him."

"Are you helping me?" Jack laughed in disbelief.

"If you wanna kill Gregory, think like him. Where would you be hiding?"

Jack turned around. After he had searched all over the house, he finally realized. Stappord turned to the couch and grinned. That's where Gregory was all along. Behind the couch …

"An ant hid," Jack hummed poorly. "But a human came and squashed it."

Jack looked at the couch and grinned. He approached. Mery grabbed the knife. The man put his knees on the couch and stretched to look behind the furniture. It was the opportune moment. Mery raised the knife and struck a blow to the back of her captor. Jack cried out in pain and collapsed to the ground. The revolver slipped across the wooden floor and stopped at the kitchen door.

"You bitch!" Jack yelled as he stood back up.

He ran toward Mery, who screamed in fear. The man grabbed her neck and began to choke her. Mery felt the air leaving her lungs. She was turning purple. Her eyes burned, and her movements started to weaken. It was the end. Suddenly there was a loud noise … followed by another and another.

Mery felt Jack's fingers loosening around her throat, and she took ragged breaths. She pulled away from Jack, who fell on the floor with three bullet holes in his back. Standing at the kitchen door, Gregory held up his enemy's gun. Mery closed her eyes in relief and kneeled.

At that moment they heard the sirens approaching. Mery looked at Gregory and smiled. He approached his neighbor and held out his hand to help her stand up. As they looked out the window, they saw an ambulance. Gregory stared at his wife, who was completely pale on the couch.

"Take care of her. I'll be arrested once the police arrive."

"You saved my life, Gregory," Mery replied. "I won't let the police take you. Samantha needs you."

Mery ran outside the house and met her family. She hugged each one and said, "We need to talk."

"What happened in there?" Carlota asked.

"We heard gunshots!" Carla commented.

"I'll tell you everything, but you must do what I say."

Mery told her family everything Jack and the others told her. Of course, some information she kept to herself—like the part where Clark was Jack Stappord's regular client and used to buy drugs.

Once Mery finished her story, the police and the paramedics arrived. The officers jumped out of their cars and ran toward Samantha's house, but the Mackenzies blocked their entrance. A few seconds later, Gregory emerged with Samantha in his arms. The paramedics came and put her on a stretcher. She was still bleeding a lot, so the medics were acting as fast as they could to save her life. When Gregory was about to enter the ambulance, some policemen held him and cuffed him.

"No!" Gregory yelled, struggling, "Let me go!"

"You can't arrest this man!" Mery said, approaching.

"Lady, step away," one of the officers said.

"He did nothing wrong! The man inside is the culprit!" Ana shouted.

"I will not ask you to step away again!" the policeman yelled in response as he dragged Gregory to the car.

"Officer, I've been a hostage in there. I know what happened!" Mery said firmly.

The officer glanced at her with a suspicious look. Gregory stopped struggling for a second and looked at his neighbor. He was scared, but he knew Mery wouldn't let him go to jail.

"Carlos," the policeman said, "put this man in the car. I'll listen to her story."

"Yes, Ramirez."

When Carlos walked away with Gregory, Ramirez turned his attention to Mery and her family. Mery breathed slowly and deeply and prepared herself to speak, but Ana was the one who spoke first. "It all started several years ago. Samantha, our neighbor and friend, started a relationship with Jack Stappord, a famous executive and also a drug dealer."

"Months later Samantha found out about Jack's extra job and met Gregory. They fell in love, and she told her new boyfriend Jack's secret," Matt explained. "Gregory is a CIA agent and decided to protect Samantha with his office's support."

"They fled," Carla told the officer. "We didn't hear from them for several years, not until they returned eighteen years later."

"Why did they come back?" Ramirez asked.

"Because they thought they were safe," Carlota answered. "During a party the mayor's wife was mysteriously shot. No one ever knew the reason until now. Jack hired a sniper to get rid of Samantha, but the guy missed the target and shot the first lady instead."

"After that, Jack killed his partner and faked his own death," Cordelia said. "Then he came back to finish things. His plan was to kill Samantha in front of Gregory so he could experience the same pain Jack felt when Gregory fled with Samantha years ago."

"Aunt Mery received a letter for Samantha by mistake," Thales said. "When she decided to return the letter, she eventually became Jack's hostage as well."

"He told me the whole story," Mery concluded. "And he said he was gonna kill me just for fun. When we called Gregory at Jack's request, he spoke with my niece so she could call the police. When Greg got to the house, he and Jack fought. Gregory hid, and I challenged Jack, who started to choke me until three shots were fired. Jack fell to the floor as Greg left his hiding place with the gun in his hand."

"How did the girl get shot?" Ramirez asked.

"She told Jack she never really loved him. So he said he would kill her now without feeling guilty. So he took the shot."

"So, Officer, the man you're driving to jail is the big hero. You've gotta release him and let him be with his wife. She needs him," Carlota said.

CHAPTER

11

Impulse

IT WAS LATE AFTERNOON ON Crystal Street. The sun was slowly disappearing down the street, leaving the sky cast with a beautiful yellowish-orange color. The night breeze began to blow, refreshing the locals after a disturbing day.

The paramedics and police officers had already left the premises, and the reporters who arrived minutes later to talk about the incident eventually went their separate ways too.

While Carla prepared dinner, Matt decided to sit on the swing on the porch of his house to relax and reflect a bit about everything his family had experienced in the last few hours. After a few minutes the boy decided it was time to go back inside, but a voice caught his attention. When he turned around, he ran into Robert climbing the porch steps and walking toward him.

"What are you doing here?"

"I came to see how you were," he answered. "I was worried—"

"Well, now you've seen me, you may go."

The boy turned around, but Robert called to his son and sat on the swing. Matt rolled his eyes and sat beside his father. They were silent for a few minutes until Robert finally said, "You may not believe me when I tell you this, but I was really worried about your aunt today. When I was with your mother, she was my favorite of all your relatives. I really liked her. Still do. And when you called to cancel dinner because something had happened, I had to come."

Matt gave a short, contemptuous, but relieved chuckle. He said nothing for a long time, and neither did Robert. After a few more minutes, a tear trickled down from the corner of the boy's eye, and he said, "I could not lose her. When I heard she was hostage at Samantha's house, all I could think about was her. I was scared."

"This is natural," Robert said with a smile. "But thank God everything went well. Samantha's out of danger. Your aunt is alive, and Gregory didn't go to jail."

"Yes—"

"You said you might need my help," Robert said, changing the subject.

"Probably," Matt said, staring at his father. "But I'm not really sure how you're gonna help me. I need to get some more information first."

"Okay. You have my number. Just call me when you have an answer."

~oOo~

Carlota was sitting in the kitchen, boiling water in a kettle. She thought about having some chamomile tea in order to sleep better after that tortuous day. Just thinking about what could've happened to her daughter gave Carlota chest pains.

When the water finally boiled, Carlota got a mug and filled it with the hot liquid. Then she put a tea bag in the cup. She waited a few minutes till the color of the water and the smell changed.

She left the mug on the kitchen counter and went to the cabinet to get some cookies when the doorbell rang. Carlota closed the cabinet and ran to open the door. When she got there, she saw someone she never expected to see—Diane Thompson. They stared at each other for several minutes until Carlota allowed the widow to come inside her house.

Diane walked to the living room and sat on the couch. She put her purse on the coffee table and waited for Carlota to walk inside. The woman came a few moments later and stood in the doorway with her arms crossed.

"I just made some tea. Do you want some?"

"Yes, that would be good. Thanks."

Carlota nodded and went to the kitchen. Diane arrived at the room a few moments later. Carlota prepared some more tea and handed a mug to the widow. They sat at the kitchen counter and were quiet once again. After twenty minutes of silence, Diane straightened in her chair and said, "Carlota, we need to talk."

"Do we?" Carlota asked. "Let's agree to disagree. Last time we spoke, you said everything you had to say to me, and I did the same. And that's how our friendship ended. What could we possibly have to say to each other? In my point of view, absolutely nothing."

"I saw the news!" Diane said at last. "I was very worried when they said Mery was a hostage. I know she's fine, but I had to see you to see how you were."

"Wow … I am lucky. Who in the world has a friend like you, Diane?" Carlota mocked. "For your information I am fine, and I don't need you to comfort me. I have my family and my chamomile tea! Now, if you would get out of my house, I'd be immensely grateful."

"Carlota, I came to apologize! All those things I said to you, I was wrong! I regret it every day."

"I don't care what you think. We're no longer friends, Diane. You can go to hell for all I care."

"Carlota—"

"I don't wanna talk to you, Diane! I thought I was able to restart our friendship, but I know you're not being completely honest with me."

"What you mean?"

"You still think I'm to blame for your husband's death," Carlota retorted. "And you are in need of someone to talk to. The problem is that the only person you have is the one you pushed away with a pointless accusation. Have you ever stopped to think that Michelle could be the killer?"

"No."

"No? So you prefer to believe that a professional whore that was screwing your husband is innocent instead of your best friend? Unbelievable."

Diane nodded and then stood up. Carlota put her head in her hands and closed her eyes. She was trembling. Perhaps out of anger or regret, maybe even a bit of both.

The widow left the kitchen. Carlota stayed there for a few more seconds until she heard the front door close. She stood up and got her cookies from the cupboard. After she put some on a plate, she grabbed her tea mug and went to her bedroom, where she remained for the rest of the day.

~oOo~

The next day Samantha woke up around nine in the morning. She was a little fuzzy from the pain medication the doctors were giving her. On the table next to her there was a tray with a glass of orange juice and two pieces of toast with grape jelly. When Samantha looked to her left, she had a surprise. Sleeping in the armchair was Mery.

Mery slowly opened her eyes and smiled. Samantha returned the gesture. They were silent for a second until Samantha asked, "What are you doing here?"

"Gregory came with you yesterday. I came this morning and told him to go to your house and get some rest," Mery explained. "I couldn't sleep at all last night."

"Oh, then you should go back to sleep."

"I'm fine. Don't worry about me. I won't sleep properly for a few more days. Being held hostage can be very traumatizing, you know?"

Samantha laughed, which caused a sharp pain in her wound. Mery stood up and gave her friend a glass of water. Samantha thanked her with a pained smile.

"Mery, I want you to know—"

"Don't talk too much," Mery said with a smile. "And you don't get to apologize for anything. We're fine."

"So that means we're friends again?"

"Yes, we're friends again."

At that moment, the bedroom door opened and a nurse walked in. Mery sat in the chair, once again making room for the Good Samaritan to approach Samantha's bed. The girl flashed a slight smile. She checked out the fluids that kept dripping down the tube and into Samantha's arm and asked, "How are you feeling today?"

"Well, but I'm still in pain," Samantha answered.

"That's normal. Painkillers are available, but I strongly advise you take them only when necessary. They can be very addictive."

"Okay."

The nurse picked up a clipboard that was hanging on the front of the bed and wrote some things down. After a few seconds she asked, "Did you eat anything today?"

"No, I just had a glass of water minutes ago."

"But you've gotta eat. It will give you more strength," the nurse said as she kept taking notes on the clipboard.

"I don't feel hungry," Samantha answered. "I've tried to eat, but I can't, not since yesterday evening."

"Hmm … I'll talk to your doctor and ask him to prescribe you some medication to whet your appetite."

"Thank you."

The nurse nodded and hung the clipboard back up. The woman said good-bye and left. Mery approached Samantha and asked, "Why don't you wanna eat?"

"I don't feel well. I'm probably still shaken up by what happened yesterday."

"Hmm … maybe. But once the doctor prescribes you the medicine, all will be well."

Mery's phone started to ring, and she got it out of her pocket. It was Cordelia. She turned to Samantha and said, "It's Cordelia. I'll answer outside. Be back in a jiffy."

"Sure, go."

Mery left the room and closed the door as she answered the phone.

"Cordelia, hi!"

"Hey, sis," Cordelia said. "I'm calling because I've received an answer regarding the lawsuit."

"Oh, that's terrific! What did they say?"

"I spoke with a friend of mine who's really close to the judge. The guy already has the paperwork. We're gonna meet in court tomorrow morning!"

"Fantastic! What time?"

"Eight o'clock. Don't be late."

"I'll be there!"

Mery hung up the phone and went back into the room. Samantha was sitting on her bed, reading a magazine. She looked up and smiled at her friend once again. Mery approached and said, "Our hearing is tomorrow!"

"What hearing?" Samantha asked, putting the magazine on her lap.

"Oh, right … you don't know about it. Cordelia and I decided to sue the rehab center, where Helena was, for negligence. If it wasn't for them, Helena would still be alive."

"Oh," Samantha said.

"I still cannot believe that it happened. But I have faith that the bastard who did this will pay! He won't get away with it."

Samantha didn't say a word. She just nodded and continued to read her magazine. Mery sat on her chair once again and started playing on her cell phone until she left when Gregory arrived a few hours later.

~oOo~

When Ana came home from work shortly after lunch, she found Thales sitting at the kitchen counter. He was eating a bowl of green grapes, but he seemed to be a little sad. She approached and gave her child a kiss on the head.

"How was your day?"

"Well," Thales replied without looking at his mother.

"It doesn't seem to have been that good. You seem upset about something. What happened?"

Thales stood up and went to the refrigerator and got a can of Coke. He opened his drink and leaned over the counter to face his mother. Ana put her purse on the chair beside her and said, "Speak."

"Sometimes life creates certain situations that make us reflect on several things. From those reflections we can get lots of things, good or bad."

"I believe that the situation you are referring to involves what happened to your aunt Mery yesterday, isn't it?" Ana asked.

"Yes," Thales said. "That's basically what I did all day. I reflected on my life, our life."

"Aren't you a bit young to do this kind of thing?"

"Don't make jokes. I'm serious. I'm sixteen, but you know I'm more mature than a lot of people your own age."

"Sorry," Ana said, smiling. "So that reflection of yours, did you get something out of it?"

"Yes."

"Good or bad?"

"Depends on the point of view," Thales explained. "What's good for me might not be for you … and vice versa."

Ana ran a hand through her hair and rested her leg on the chair she'd put her purse on earlier. Thales took a sip of his soda and said nothing. Mother and son stared at each other for several minutes until Ana asked, "What I'll say is no joke, but you're really scaring me with this pep talk. What did you get from your reflection?"

"A few weeks ago, more like in the beginning of July—"

"Over a month ago," Ana said. "What happened?"

"Matt and I had a conversation, but I made him promise that he'd tell no one what I told him," Thales replied. "After what happened yesterday and my reflection today, I see that Matt was right, and I have to tell you the truth."

"Thales, please say it. I'm scared!"

"Mom … I'm gay."

Ana was quiet for a moment. She stood up and walked toward her son. Her eyes sparkled. Thales realized at that moment that his mother was making a decision. She was disappointed, but he had to tell her the truth. Would he get spanked? Disinherited?

"I—" Ana started as she got closer to her son. "I am so happy you've told me."

"What!" Thales asked in shock.

"I was hoping you'd tell me this a long time ago! I'm so glad that you finally opened up to me."

"You knew? Did Matt say something?" Thales asked, irritated.

"No, he didn't say anything. But a mother knows her child, and I've always known you were gay. And believe me,

I don't care. I love you, and I will always love you. If that's your choice, if that's who you are, I couldn't be happier."

"Will you tell the family?"

"Oh no," Ana answered. "They already know. I'll just tell them that you opened up, and they'll be very happy."

Ana kissed her son and exited the kitchen. Thales stood there, holding his soda can, completely awestruck. But deep down he felt relieved about finally telling his mother the truth, even though she had already known.

~oOo~

Adriana was sitting on the couch reading a magazine when she heard the doorbell ring. She rolled her eyes and put the magazine on the cushion and went to receive the visitor. When she opened the door, she saw Matt standing outside.

"Matt? What are you doing here? I haven't seen you in days."

"I came for a visit," the boy answered with a smile.

"Oh, you can come in if you want, but Clark and your mother left awhile ago," Adriana replied.

"I know."

Adriana raised an eyebrow and allowed the boy's entry. Matt went to the living room and stood before a table on the opposite wall from the couch. He was analyzing some pictures when Adriana arrived.

"What is this visit about?"

"I came to see you," Matt answered. "Because I have a question that's stuck in my head."

"I'm curious."

"Whenever I come here, I look at this photo, but I never found out who this lady is, the one next to Clark."

"Ah, that's Susan," Adriana answered. "Clark's sister."

"And where is she now?"

"Matt, why are you asking me this?"

"Because you live here and you know the family," Matt replied. "Given the fact that there's a room upstairs filled with women clothes, I assume she's dead, am I right?"

"No," Adriana finally said, "she's very much alive."

Matt turned around and took a deep breath. His greatest fear became reality. Mery and Cordelia were right when they discovered Susan's whereabouts. Adriana was silent for several minutes until Matt turned to her and said, "Why would Clark tell my mother his sister is dead when she's alive?"

"I can't tell you," Adriana said. "But I can tell you where to find her."

"But—"

"Shh. If I tell you something and Clark finds out, I'll end up dead. For that reason it is better if you talk to someone who's already *dead*."

"She's at the rehab center, isn't she?" Matt asked.

"Yes," Adriana replied. "Go there. Room 320. But remember, Clark paid all the staff at that place. Don't forget your wallet."

"I have thought about that."

Matt ran toward the front door and turned the knob, but before he left, he faced Adriana and asked, "Why have you decided to help me?"

"I will not let you go through the same suffering I went through," she said. "I wasn't able to save my parents, but you'll save your mother."

CHAPTER
12

Susan and Clark

PHOTOGRAPHERS AND REPORTERS SURROUNDED THE place. As people were leaving the courtroom, the media vultures advanced. The audience members at the hearing were blinded for several seconds because of the flashes. Some of the people stumbled. Others fell down the stairs, but the press continued to advance.

Their goal was to reach the stars of the trial—the heroes, the villains, and the judge. The heroes were Mery and Cordelia Mackenzie. The villains were Dr. Price and his companion, Dr. Parker. The judge was the Honorable Edgar Dunning.

When one of the reporters reached the courtroom, Judge Dunning made the security guards remove him, and then he had them remove the rest of the press.

The trial took three days to be concluded, and after an arduous battle of evidence from both sides, the Mackenzie sisters finally won and gave Helena the justice she deserved, at least that's what they thought.

In one corner of the room, Dr. Price and Dr. Parker sat, totally discredited. Mery and Cordelia approached the men with stamped smiles on their faces. Dr. Price stood and said, "You won! Congratulations!"

"But don't get too excited," Dr. Parker said. "Happiness is short-lived."

"You shouldn't treat us like that," Cordelia said and laughed. "You have nothing else to brag about. Unless you think that losing your medical license is something great. I don't think it is."

"You two will pay for this!" Dr. Price shouted, enraged.

"Oh no, Doctor," Mery said. "You two paid. We owe nothing more."

The two psychiatrists turned around and left the court. The sisters hugged and looked up as if to communicate with Helena. The women went to their seats and gathered their things. When they were about to leave, the judge called for them.

"I would like to speak with Cordelia," the judge said.

"Well, I'm all ears," Cordelia said and smiled.

"I was wondering if by any chance you'd like to go to dinner with me."

"Oh my God!" Mery said before she burst into laughter. "Of course she'd like to! Say yes!"

"Mery!" Cordelia said, scolding her sister. "Don't answer for me!"

"If you don't wanna go, I'll understand perfectly," Edgar Dunning said, saddened.

"Of course I accept, Judge," Cordelia replied. "It would be a pleasure."

~oOo~

Adriana was taking a nap on the couch when she heard the front door close violently. She heard the hurried steps and Clark's heavy breathing. The woman sat up slowly and stared at her old boss with some doubt. The man approached her and said angrily, "Don't just stand there. Get me a drink!"

"If you wanna drink, get it yourself. I no longer work for you, remember?" Adriana asked, lying down again.

"Since when do you talk to me like this? With this … this insolence?"

Adriana rose to her feet, fuming with rage. Her eyes were red, and her facial expression was enough to leave anyone terrified. She stared at Clark and yelled, "From the day you bought drugs and spent all your money on it! From the day you told me you were poor and couldn't afford my salary anymore, even though we had a deal!"

"Had?" Clark asked. "I don't remember our deal being scrapped."

Clark approached his former maid and grabbed her chin. Adriana stifled a scream and stared at the man. They were both filled with rage, but Adriana was the only one who was afraid.

"Pay close attention," Clark said. "If you break our agreement, I will kill you before you say anything to the police."

"Go ahead. Kill me," Adriana said and laughed. "It would not be the first time for you. And if you kill me, it won't go unpunished. People will find out who you are either through me or through you. It's been fifteen years since what you did. The loss of your money was just the beginning of your suffering. And now that Jack Stappord's really dead, you have no chance to recover what once belonged to you."

"How do you know he's dead?" Clark asked, releasing her.

"I may not have your same degree of education, Clark, but I do watch the news. Isn't that why you're angry? Because you're starting to see what the world is doing to you? Clark, get ready because soon … everything will collapse."

Adriana turned around and walked away from the man. When she was halfway up the staircase, Clark called for her. Adriana stopped, but she didn't turn around to face her former employer.

"What makes you think that if you tell my secret, you won't be arrested as well for what you did?"

"Oh, Clark, did I ever say that I wasn't going to turn myself in once I turned you in?" Adriana laughed as she walked up the stairs.

~oOo~

The car stopped right in front of the Greendale Rehab Center. Robert turned off the vehicle and turned to Matt, who seemed nervous. They were silent for a while until the man asked, "Can I at least know what we're doing here?"

"I hope you brought a good amount of money."

"Matt, look, I will never complain about helping you, but I need to understand what's going on."

"I don't have time to explain," the boy answered. "Let's go."

Matt stepped out of the car and walked toward the building. Robert followed his son, and they met at the reception area. The nurse responsible for the place was on the phone, but once she realized the presence of the visitors, she ended her conversation.

"How can I help you?" she asked with a kind smile.

"I'd like to visit Susan Abromheit."

"Oh, I'm sorry, but we don't have any patients with that name," the woman answered.

"I know you do. How much money did Clark give you to lie about his sister? We're ready to give you more if it's needed," Matt replied.

~oOo~

She was sitting on the couch in front of the window. Her expression was one of joy, probably because of the beauty of the garden or perhaps because of her mental issues. But Susan Abromheit seemed like a happy woman. At least that was what Matt thought once he entered the lady's room.

He approached the woman, and she smiled broadly. Susan stood up and asked the boy to sit on the bed. He obeyed and sat down. They were silent for a little while until Susan asked with her sweet, relaxing voice, "Who are you?"

"My name is Matt Mackenzie. I'm friends with Adriana, your maid."

"Oh—" Susan said.

At that moment the woman's facial expression completely changed. Her smile turned sour and contemptuous. She sat down and motioned for Matt to continue his story. The boy cleared his throat and took a deep breath.

"I met Adriana a few months ago when my mother started dating your brother."

"Matt, I won't interrupt you anymore, but I ask you, please," Susan said, "don't ever refer to Clark as my brother. He stopped being my brother a long time ago when he threw me into this hellhole."

"But you seemed happy."

"I have to do something not to go crazy," she explained. "Imagining that this place is paradise is my best option. It was something that I improved over time. But please … go on."

"My mom started dating Clark. Ever since the beginning of the relationship I wasn't fond of him. One day I found bricks of cocaine at the mansion, and Adriana subtly confirmed that they belonged to Clark. I tried to warn my mother, but it was a foolish attempt. Then my girlfriend and I found a box in your room indicating that someone would kill the mayor. He died later that night at a party. Clark was there."

"Oh my God!" Susan exclaimed. "Have you told anyone about this?"

"No, I was scared," Matt replied. "If Clark's capable of murder, he could do so much worse to me and my mom."

Susan ran her hands through her hair and stood up. She walked to the opposite window and leaned against the sill to admire the beautiful landscape that existed behind the building. After a few minutes, Susan turned around to face the boy once again.

"What did Adriana tell you?"

"Not much," Matt said. "She just told me where to find you."

"So I guess you came here looking for answers."

"Yes," Matt said, standing up. "Please, Ms. Abromheit, I need your help."

"Call me Susan."

"Susan, please."

The woman nodded and motioned for the boy to sit. Matt returned to his seat and shook his head. Susan stepped forward and began her story.

"What I'm about to tell you occurred fifteen years ago."

"Okay."

"I came home one day and found my dad crying on the couch. Adriana stood beside him, but once she noticed my presence, she withdrew from the living room. After a few minutes of conversation with my dad, I found out that Clark had interdicted him."

"What?"

"Clark was responsible for my dad's power of attorney," Susan explained. "He made everyone believe that my father had serious mental problems. Clark and I got into a terrible fight that night. As a result, he locked me in here and gave away a large sum of money so no one could see me except for Adriana."

"And did she come to visit you?" Matt asked.

"A couple of times. During one of her visits she told me that Clark told everyone that my father had freaked out and killed me. He said I was cremated and my ashes were thrown in a creek. A few days later Adriana came back and told me that Mom and Dad had died. I cried for days. But I couldn't leave. For fifteen years I've been nourished by these nurses, and I've never taken any medication, not once. They all know I'm not sick, but because of the money, they keep their mouths shut."

"Susan, I had no idea," Matt said in shock. "I am so sorry."

"No one has," Susan said and laughed. "And don't be sorry for me, boy. At least I'm far away from that gold-digging bastard. Now you must go and save your mother."

"I will save you too."

"Oh, Matt, I don't think anyone will be able to do that."

"I promise I'll get you out. Thanks for the answers."

When Matt walked out of the room, he met his father standing in the hallway. The man ran to his son and asked, "Did you get what you wanted?"

"I did. Now take me home. I need to tell Mom!"

"You got it!"

CHAPTER

13

Dark Past

ROBERT PARKED HIS CAR RIGHT in front of Matt's house. The boy left the vehicle and ran toward his home with his father on his heels. When the boy was about to open the door to the house, he heard someone calling his name. He turned around and saw his aunt Mery approaching, breathless.

She was wearing a gym suit, and her hair was pulled back with a rubber band. She greeted Robert and walked closer to her nephew. The two crept into a corner of the porch, and Mery asked, "Did you go to the rehab center?"

"Yes, you were right. Clark's sister is alive."

"Oh my God!" Mery exclaimed as she jogged in place. "What are you gonna do?"

"I'll tell Mom."

Matt turned toward the door, but his aunt grabbed him. She pulled him closer and whispered in his ear, "Don't forget to tell her that Clark was Jack Stappord's best customer."

"What?" Matt asked. "So that explains the cocaine."

"You knew about the drugs?"

"Yeah, I told Mom, but she wouldn't listen. Now I'll tell her everything I know. I gotta end this."

Matt hugged his aunt and entered the house. He called for his mother, who did not respond. He ran to the living room, and there she was, sitting on the couch and watching television.

"What's all that racket?" she asked, staring at the boy.

"Mom, we need to talk! It's urgent."

"Hello, Matt," a voice said.

Matt was paralyzed. He turned around to face the owner of that voice. And to his sorrow and despair, the voice belonged to Clark. The man approached the boy, who stepped back and asked, "Clark, what are you doing here?"

"I came to visit your mother," he answered. "And I couldn't help but hear that you have something important to say. May I ask what it is?"

"Umm ... sorry, but it's something that I must work on with my mom."

"Of course. I understand," Clark said. "It was a short visit anyway. I'm leaving now. Bye, honey!"

"Bye," Carla replied, standing up. "Will I see you later?"

"Surely."

At that moment the front door opened, and Robert walked in. Clark's eyes widened almost instantly. He looked at Robert and Matt, and then he turned to Carla. Silence filled the room until Robert said, "Hello, Clark."

"What the hell is this man doing here?"

~oOo~

When the door to the room opened, Samantha looked up to face the nurse that was carrying a tray with her lunch. Samantha smiled as she put her book on the table beside her and made room for the Good Samaritan to put the tray on her lap.

"Here's your lunch, Mrs. Desmond."

"Thanks, Bertha."

The woman left the room, and Samantha was alone once again. She uncovered her food and started to eat. As beautiful as the presentation of the dish was, the grub was terrible. The noodles seemed burned and undercooked at the same time, while the steak was dry and charred.

Samantha winced and covered the tray again. She carried the object and placed it next to her book. And then the bedroom door opened yet again, and Gregory came inside. Samantha smiled at the sight of her husband. He approached and gave her a passionate kiss.

"I'm glad you came," Samantha said once their lips were separate. "We need to talk about something important. Lock the door."

Gregory obeyed his wife and locked the door. He pulled a chair closer to the bed and sat down next to his wife. Samantha pulled her hair back into a bun. She breathed deeply and slowly till she said, "Remember when I told you that Mery and Cordelia filed a lawsuit against the rehab center?"

"Yes … what about it?"

"They won!"

"Are you serious?" Gregory asked, grinning.

"Yes, they've won! That means we can finally stop worrying, because now everyone will blame the psychiatrists for Helena's death!" Samantha cheered.

"Thank God!" Gregory said and then laughed.

Gregory stood and went to the fridge. He got himself a glass of water and returned to his seat. He stared at his wife for several minutes until she asked with a mischievous smile, "What?"

"Do you know that I love you?"

"I love you, Greg."

~oOo~

The four people were completely silent for more than ten minutes. Clark's eyes were red with anger. Matt was trembling, afraid of what his mother's boyfriend's next move could be. Carla had absolutely no reaction. Meanwhile, Robert was the only one who remained calm.

"Answer me!" Clark finally yelled. "What's this man doing here?"

"I don't know," Carla said. "I really don't know."

"Liar! Are you fucking him? Huh? Answer me!"

Carla slapped him then. Clark stepped back and covered his face with his hand. He looked at his girlfriend with even more anger. Carla approached him and said, "The very next time you suggest I'm having an affair, I will leave you."

"I just want answers. One day you say you hate this man, but the next day he's walking into your house."

"Don't forget that this is my house as well!" Matt said, stepping forward. "And this man is my father, meaning that he can walk in here whenever he wants."

Carla's eyes widened, and she looked at Matt, completely surprised. Robert took a deep breath and gave a slight smile as his eyes filled with tears of joy. This was the first time Matt had referred to him as a father, at least honestly.

"He's not your father, Matt. He left you!"

"People make mistakes!" Matt replied. "Yes, he left, but now he's here trying to redeem himself."

"And he succeeded?" Carla asked.

"Not yet," Matt answered. "Now Clark, if you allow me, I'd like to speak to my parents alone."

Clark rolled his eyes. Carla's handprint was stamped on Clark's face. He approached his girlfriend and gave her a kiss on the cheek. She did not resist it, but she didn't return the gesture either. When Clark left the house, Matt turned to his mother and said, "We need to talk."

"I can't talk right now," she said, turning around.

"Carla!" Robert said as his ex-wife faced him. "Listen to the boy! He has an important thing to tell you!"

"Can you wait outside?" Matt asked.

"Yes, I've got some business that needs my attendance."

Robert eventually left the house. Matt and Carla stared at each other quietly. Matt approached his mother and reached for her. She took her son's hand, and they walked to the living room together and sat on the couch.

"What do you wanna talk about?"

"Mother, I discovered some stuff today that might shock you. I need you to stay calm and listen to everything I've gotta tell you."

"Matt, you're scaring me," Carla said. "What did you find out?"

"Where's Clark's sister?" Matt asked.

"What do you mean by that? Susan died years ago."

"That's where you're wrong. Susan Abromheit is very much alive."

Carla raised an eyebrow. She released her son's hand and backed off a bit. Matt looked into his mother's eyes and said, "On the day that Grandma and Aunt Mery went to the rehab center to talk about the lawsuit, they discovered the existence of a patient. Her name? Susan Abromheit."

"That's not possible," Carla said. "She must be another woman."

"That's what I thought when they told me. But since I had many doubts about Clark, I could not leave this information alone. I had to know the truth. I went to the mansion, and I spoke with Adriana. She told me that Susan is still alive and that she's a *patient* at the Greendale Rehab Center."

"Oh my God." Carla stood up and ran her hand through her hair. She was trembling. The woman began to walk from one side of the room to the other, sighing. Matt remained in his seat, observing his mother's movements.

"That … that's a lie!" Carla yelled.

"I wish it was," Matt commented. "I called Dad, and he took me to the center. Clark paid nurses and doctors so they wouldn't reveal Susan's existence. We paid some people, and I was able to talk to her."

"You spoke with Susan?"

"I did … She told me her story—how she got home and found out that Clark had lied about their father's mental issues and how he had gotten power of attorney. Then Susan told me about the fight she and her brother had that night and how he had put her in the car and admitted her to the rehab center."

"No, I cannot believe this!" Carla said with tears in her eyes. "Why would Clark lie to me?"

"I don't know," Matt answered as he approached his mother. "But that's why you've gotta get rid of him. He's dangerous."

"Matt, please tell me you're lying."

"I'm not. I am so sorry."

"I've gotta talk to Adriana. I'm going to the mansion," Carla concluded and then ran out of the room.

"No, you're not going alone!" Matt said. He grabbed ahold of his mother, but she pushed him against the wall.

"Don't follow me! Stay here!"

Carla grabbed her car keys and left. Matt stood there for a few seconds, astonished. He got his phone and texted Sarah. Then he grabbed his car keys and also left the house.

~oOo~

Adriana was preparing some instant noodles in the kitchen when she heard the doorbell ring several times. She turned off the microwave and ran to open the door. Once she turned the knob, Carla walked into the house. Carla stopped in the middle of the living room and leaned against the couch.

"Hey, Carla, I'm sorry, but Clark's not home. If you wanna wait, please be my guest."

"What happened to Clark's sister?" Carla asked without hesitation.

"Why don't you ask him that?"

"Just answer the goddamn question!"

Adriana swallowed. She closed the door and walked toward Carla. Both were quiet for a short period of time, and then the maid said, "What do you wanna know exactly?"

"Everything," Carla replied. "Matt told me a crazy story. I need a confirmation."

"Okay," Adriana said. "But you may wanna sit."

Carla nodded and sat down on the couch. Adriana sat on the chair in front of the fireplace. Carla put her belongings on the table and motioned for Adriana to continue.

"Several years ago when I was nine, my father decided to run for public office. He was at the top. My mom and I were really proud. My father's vice—"

"I'm sorry, but what does this have to do with what I wanna know?" Carla asked.

"I'll get there."

"Sorry. Carry on."

"My father's vice was a man called David Thompson. They were the best of friends. At least that's what Dad thought. In the end David threw my dad's name in the mud, and he was humiliated and rejected by all those who once loved him. Thompson got the job instead, and my father lost all his money. My mother was so devastated she succumbed to alcoholism. A few months later she died of cirrhosis."

"Oh my God."

"The day of the funeral, my dad was unable to leave the house, so I went alone with the neighbors. When I came back home, I found my dad lying in bed amid a pool of blood with a bullet hole in his head," Adriana said.

"Adriana, I had no idea. I am so sorry," Carla replied, resting her hands on her chest.

"After that, I went to an orphanage. But nobody wanted to adopt me, so when I turned eighteen, I started working as a maid. I went through several households until I met my future husband. But it didn't last long. When he found out I couldn't have kids, he left. Seventeen years later Victor Abromheit hired me."

Adriana stood up and motioned for Carla to follow her. They went to the kitchen. The maid poured a glass of water for herself and another one for her visitor. The women sat down at the table, and Adriana continued. "Time passed. One day I was here in the kitchen, looking for some things I kept in a box. I thought I was alone, but Clark caught me. I didn't think he would care, but then he saw David Thompson's picture and the map."

"Map?" Carla asked. "What map?"

"I broke into David's house one night and made a map," Adriana explained. "When Clark saw the map, he confronted me, and I told him my story. At that moment, I realized I was doomed and going to jail, but Clark didn't say a word. A few weeks later a fight broke out. Clark managed to get a fake certificate stating that Mr. Abromheit suffered from several mental problems and couldn't handle the expenses anymore."

"What did Clark do?" Carla asked before she took a sip of her water.

"He took his father's power of attorney. Now Clark was responsible for all the finances. Susan came home that night and found out about everything. She and her brother had a terrible fight. Clark put her in the car and drove her to the clinic. He paid a good amount of money so no one would mention her whereabouts."

"So Matt was right?"

"Since the beginning. When Clark came home that day, he told his parents everything. Mrs. Abromheit was so shocked that she had a heart attack and died. Mr. Abromheit was so angry he got the gun he kept in the bedroom and pointed it at Clark. But the latter was faster and retrieved the weapon he used to shoot his father in the forehead."

Carla froze. Her eyes were filled with tears. The glass slipped from her hand and shattered on the floor. Adriana just sat there, staring at her boss's girlfriend. Carla opened her mouth and asked, "Clark killed his own father?"

"Yes, I saw everything. Clark said that if I told the police about him, he'd tell them about my secret. So we made a deal. We hid all the evidence and lived in silence for fifteen years—that is, until Diane Thompson had her annual gala and hired me to serve the party."

"Oh my God. You killed the mayor!" Carla said. She stood up and covered her mouth with her hands.

"Yes, I did."

Adriana approached Carla. She tried to back away, but the maid held her. They were silent for a few minutes. Carla was shaky and sweaty just like Adriana.

"Yes, I killed him," the maid said. "But I am not a bad person!"

"What does that make you then?" Carla asked.

"I was avenging my parents! I didn't want money. I wanted justice! I don't regret anything, but I feel guilty every single day."

"Guilty?"

"I waited fifteen years to get my revenge," Adriana explained. "While I waited, Clark tricked several women.

They paid for everything while he didn't spend a dime. Many lives were ruined, and I let it happen."

Adriana walked away. She got a cloth and knelt to clean up the broken glass. Carla leaned against the kitchen counter. Adriana walked through a door and came back minutes later without the cloth.

"What made you wanna help my child?"

"During these months you and Clark dated, I grew really fond of you and your son, especially after he found the cocaine in the bathroom."

"Wait. What?"

"Clark was a consumer, one of Jack Stappord's regulars."

"Oh God—"

"When everyone thought Jack had died, Clark was happy. But then he suddenly appeared and collected all the money Clark owed him for the drugs. So Clark was broke and had no money to pay me anymore."

"So that was your motivation?"

"That too," the maid explained. "But just like I said before, I really grew fond of your son. And I could not allow him to experience the same pain I did when I lost my parents. You were entering a dangerous place, Carla. And I would not let Matt lose you."

"What do you suggest?" Carla asked.

"We should call the police."

"If we tell them the truth, you will go to jail."

"Oh, Carla," Adriana said and laughed. "I never thought I'd get away with it. And after all I've done, going to jail is my best option."

"So what do we tell them?"

"Say that Clark's a murderer and that you need help!" Matt said as he walked into the kitchen.

Carla turned around and faced her son. The boy was serious and had his arms crossed. Carla's eyes were filled with tears, and she ran to hug her son. Matt hugged his mother, and she started to cry. She said between sobs, "I'm sorry. I really am sorry. I should've trusted you since the beginning."

"I forgive you. But that's a warning for you to listen to me if you ever meddle in any shit like that."

The boy let go of his mother and walked toward Adriana. The maid gave a sheepish smile and approached the boy while she reached out her hand to greet the boy. Matt pulled the woman's hand, brought her to him, and hugged her. Adriana was still, but she hugged the boy in return and shed a few tears.

"Thank you ... for everything," Matt said.

"You're welcome."

When Matt and Adriana parted, Sarah entered the kitchen. She had a shoe box in her hands. She gave the object to her boyfriend. She then hugged Carla. Adriana looked at the box for a while and said, "So you were the ones that got into the closet?"

"How do you know?" Sarah asked.

"I've cleaned this house for seventeen years, and that room has never been so full of dust before," Adriana said and laughed.

"Well, we found the box, and we know what Clark did," Matt said, looking at his mother. "Mom, inside this box there's proof that Clark killed the mayor."

"Actually, Matt," Carla replied, "this box belongs to Adriana."

"What?" the boy exclaimed as he turned to the maid.

"Yes, I killed the mayor."

"Adriana, oh my God."

At that moment, Carla sat in a chair and told her son the whole story. At the end both Matt and Sarah were completely shocked. Matt turned to his mother and said, "We gotta call the police. I always knew he was a bad person, but I never thought he was capable of so much."

Adriana picked up the phone and dialed 911. She asked them for help, and according to the operator, they'd take about twenty minutes to get to Clark's house. Adriana hung up and turned to the group.

"Now let's wait."

"Shall we go to the living room?" Matt suggested.

The group agreed, and they all went to the living room. Matt and Sarah sat on the couch, holding each other while Carla sat in a chair. Adriana decided to stand up and look out the window. The weather was closing in. A storm was coming.

After a few minutes, they heard the first thunder. The noise was so loud that it made the house vibrate. A few portraits dropped to the floor. And then the rain started. Silence dominated the living room, except for the sound of the raindrops on the roof.

"I'm getting sleepy," Sarah commented.

"You can sleep if you want."

Adriana closed the curtains and rubbed her arms with her hands. She was cold. She then grabbed a blanket that Clark kept on a trunk next to the couch. She sat on a chair and covered herself. Carla ran a hand through her hair and asked, "How was the weather that night?"

"It was a very warm day, and the sunset was beautiful," Adriana replied.

"Is this a bad sign?" Matt asked.

"No," Adriana said.

When Adriana finished her sentence, the mansion's doors opened, and Clark entered. He was all wet because of the rain. He closed the door and went to the living room. He was startled when he saw everyone sitting there.

"Carla!" he said in excitement. "It's good to see you. I thought you wouldn't come here today."

"Yeah, well … I came," she replied.

Matt and Sarah stood up and greeted the man, and so did Adriana. He looked at the group and said cheerfully, "Let's have dinner! Let's celebrate this merry gathering!"

"We can't," Carla said as she walked up to the counter of photos. "Someone's missing."

Adriana walked slowly to the kitchen and closed the door. Matt and Sarah decided to step back and get closer to the window. Clark looked confused. He approached Carla and asked:

"What do you mean that someone's missing?"

"Your sister. She's not here. You should invite her to dinner," Carla replied.

Clark's expression changed completely. He looked extremely sad, like he was about to cry. His eyes were filled with tears the moment he sat on the couch. He put his hand on his heart. Carla turned to him and offered a sly smile.

"I cannot believe I'm hearing this from you," Clark said in disappointment. "I told you my sister is dead. If this is a joke, it is in extremely bad taste."

"Oh no, Clark, this is not a joke. I'm serious."

"Carla, stop it!" Clark said, standing up. "You're annoying me."

"I believe that if you wanna have a more lively celebration, you should pick up the phone and call the rehab center to invite your sister. Or do you really think that after fifteen years of isolation she wouldn't like to be back home?"

Clark widened his eyes and took a few steps back. Matt and Sarah glanced at each other. Carla flashed a mischievous smile and walked around the room. Clark followed his girlfriend with his eyes and asked, "What did you say?"

"Yes, Clark, I know what you did. I know how you locked your sister in that clinic. I know how you recently became poor, and I also know how you got the gun and killed your own father. Aren't you gonna say anything?"

"How did you—"

"I told her," Matt said. "It was easy actually. I found some clues, and then I discovered the existence of a *patient* at the rehab center, so I went to talk to her."

"You couldn't! I paid those people! No one could've visited her!"

"You're not the only one who knows how to handle money, Clark." Matt laughed. "That's what my father was doing at my house. He drove me to the clinic. He knows everything. You are finished."

"It was Adriana, wasn't it?" Clark yelled. "She broke our deal!"

Clark ran toward the kitchen. He was too angry. Carla got in his way, but Clark grabbed her and pushed her away. She fell and hit her head on the corner of a table. Matt and Sarah ran toward her as Clark entered the kitchen.

"Mom, are you okay?"

"Ah," Carla said, stroking her bleeding forehead. "I'm a little dizzy. Wait. Adriana!"

"Stay here!" Matt said as he looked at Sarah.

"Be careful!"

Matt stood up and ran to the kitchen. When he got there, he found Adriana walking backward as Clark stepped toward her with a knife. She raised her arms in fear. Clark was sweaty, and he snorted with rage. He took two more steps and said, "You broke our deal."

"Our deal was broken long ago," Adriana said. "You might as well just go ahead and kill me. But like I've said, you won't get away with it. I've called the police!"

"When they arrive, I'll be long gone!" Clark said and laughed.

"I don't think so."

Clark turned around, and Matt hit him with a pan. The man stifled a scream and collapsed to the ground, unconscious. Adriana sighed in relief. She and Matt teamed up and dragged Clark out of the kitchen. They put him in a chair and went to help Carla, who was still bleeding.

"I'll get a wet cloth and a first-aid kit. We gotta clean that," Sarah said.

"I have a kit in my old room," Adriana replied. "You can go and pick it up. I'm getting something upstairs."

Sarah ran to the kitchen, and Adriana climbed the staircase to the upper floor. Carla touched her wound and looked at her son. Matt grinned and asked, "Are you okay?"

"Yes," she answered, "I'll be fine."

Sarah returned to the living room with a cloth and the first-aid kit. She ran the wet cloth gently on Carla's forehead to clean the blood. She then took some stuff out of the white box and said, "This may sting a bit."

"Okay."

Sarah smeared the remedy on her wound, and Carla let out a moan of pain. Matt put his hand on his mother's shoulder and gave her two gentle slaps. That was when Adriana came back to the living room with Mr. Abromheit's gun in her hand.

"Oh my God!" Sarah said when she saw the gun.

"Do you think this is necessary?" Carla asked.

"Yes," Adriana replied.

"I agree," Matt said and nodded. "We don't want him to wake up and try to fight back."

"No, you sure wouldn't want that," Clark said and laughed as he opened his eyes. "It would be terrible."

Adriana clicked the safety off on the gun and pointed it at her boss. Matt, Sarah, and Carla retreated. The man continued laughing and said, "You know, seeing you all afraid of me reminds me of my father on the day he died."

"You're sick!" Carla said. "I don't know what I was thinking when I started dating you."

When Carla completed her sentence, they heard several sirens approaching. Matt could see the red and blue lights through the window. There were at least three cars. The boy smiled and then glanced at Clark. The laughing man suddenly fell silent. For the first time Clark was scared.

"It's over Clark," Adriana said. "You've lost."

"No, not just yet!"

Clark grinned and jumped on Adriana. Carla cried out in fright. Adriana struggled, trying to pull herself away from

Clark, but he was too strong. Matt ran toward them, but he stopped when Clark pointed the gun at him.

"Yeah, go back to your place," Clark mockingly said.

"Clark! Don't do this!" Carla said.

"Shut up, woman!"

The sound of sirens grew closer. Matt stepped back and went over to Sarah, who was shaking in fear. Adriana crawled to the boy's side. Clark ran to the door and locked it. He returned to the living room and saw Carla standing beside the couch. He approached her and pointed his revolver at her, but she did not move.

"Go back there, or I'll shoot you!"

"You won't kill me," Carla said.

"Yes, I will!"

"No, you won't," Carla said and laughed. "Because you're afraid. You know that this is the end."

"No, it's not!" Clark said tearfully. "It can't be! I fought too hard to get everything I wanted. It cannot end like this!"

"Look at the chaos you've created! You locked your sister away and gave her up for dead. You murdered your own father. Do you really think this was the right way to get everything you wanted most?"

There was a knock on the door.

"It's the police! Open up!" an officer said on the other side.

"Do the right thing, Clark! For once in your life."

The man shed a few more tears. The officer continued pounding on the door. Carla smiled and wiped Clark's face. He slowly lowered his gun and sighed in relief.

"Now give me the gun," Carla said. "And we will open the door. You're gonna do the right thing."

Clark nodded and wiped his tears. Carla looked at him and extended her hand to get the gun, but Clark stepped back.

"This wouldn't be the right thing."

"C'mon, Clark. Gimme the gun," Carla said nervously.

"Open the door!" the policeman said.

"I can't give it to you," Clark replied. "It wouldn't be right."

"Yes, it would! Clark, please!"

Clark nodded and pointed the gun to his head. Carla reached out and shouted, "Clark, no!"

The man smiled one more time and took the shot. Adriana screamed at the sight of her boss falling on the floor—dead. Carla covered her mouth and closed her eyes as the police broke down the mansion's doors.

CHAPTER
14

The Good Things in Life

THE PARAMEDICS CARRIED THE BODY to the ambulance right after the rain stopped. The reporters started to arrive with their cameras and microphones. Besides them, the neighbors also gathered to find out what had happened at the Abromheit manor. Everyone was absolutely shocked when they discovered that Clark had killed himself, and even more shocked when they heard the whole story.

Matt, Carla, and Sarah were standing in front of the mansion, giving their statements to the police. Adriana was a little distant, staring at the construction. The policeman approached her and asked, "Are you Adriana?"

"Yes," she replied, crestfallen.

"You are—"

"She knows," Matt said, walking toward the officer. "I'd appreciate if you could give us a minute."

The man shook his head and walked away. The group followed Adriana to a corner where there wasn't much movement. The maid was in tears, but she still managed a smile. Sarah got a handkerchief out of her pocket and gave it to the woman, and she wiped her face. Carla approached Adriana and said, "What you did was the right thing."

"I know," Adriana replied, laughing. "But you guys helped me."

"Thank you, Adriana. You really are a good person."

Carla walked away, and Sarah accompanied her. Adriana glanced at Matt for a second and said, "Don't do it. It will only make things worse."

"You think so?" he asked and laughed. "Sometimes a hug helps."

He wrapped her in a hug, and she returned the gesture with many tears. When they parted, the maid dried her face once again. The boy smiled for a while and said, "Thank you. From the bottom of my heart, thank you. You helped to save my mother, and nothing I say or do will be able to repay what you did for me."

"Just don't stop being my friend," Adriana said. "You can repay me like that."

"I can do that. And I promise to visit you whenever I can."

Adriana didn't respond. She just smiled and walked away. She approached the officer and prodded him on the shoulder.

"I'm ready."

The policeman shook his head and handcuffed her. Adriana entered the car and looked at the Abromheit's manor one last time. The driver started the engine, and the vehicle started to move away slowly until Adriana could no longer see the house she had worked in for so long.

~oOo~

Diane Thompson rang the bell and waited a few seconds until Carlota opened the door. They stared at each other until Carlota asked impatiently, "What are you doing here?"

Diane did not respond. Carlota rolled her eyes and started to close the door, but the widow prevented her from doing so. Diane stared at her friend for a second and was about to say something when Carlota yelled, "Either you answer my question, or I'll turn around and slam the door in your face."

The mayor's widow nodded and did something that Carlota never expected her to do. Diane knelt and clasped her hands in front of her, as if she was praying. Carlota rolled her eyes once again and stared at her friend.

"Please, Carlota. Forgive me. What I did was very wrong. I should've been a better friend. I should've trusted you!"

"Yes, you should have. You saw the news, didn't you?"

"Yes, I have," Diane said with tears in her eyes. "I am sorry that I accused you! I've messed up, and I admit my mistake!"

"Do you wanna cup of coffee?"

"That … that'd be nice."

Carlota smiled and helped her friend stand up. Diane laughed and hugged her friend. They went to the kitchen, where Carlota brewed some coffee. Then Carlota brought a container with some cookies she had baked earlier.

"So you forgive me?"

"What do you think?" Carlota said and laughed. "You're my oldest friend. Of course I forgive you. Besides, in all true friendships there are moments of hardship, but in the end everything goes back to normal."

Diane smiled and sipped her coffee. Carlota took some cookies and put them on a napkin in front of her. The women continued chatting, and before they knew it, it was eight o'clock at night. The mayor's widow decided it was time to go home. Carlota accompanied her friend to the door, and they scheduled dinner for the beginning of the next week.

~oOo~

It was about the same time Diane left Carlota's house when Cordelia heard the horn. She looked out the window and saw the black BMW parked in front of her house. She grinned and ran to the dresser. Cordelia combed her hair and put on a red lipstick. She grabbed her black shiny purse that was on the bed and went downstairs.

When Cordelia left her house, Judge Edgar Dunning was standing outside, leaning against his car. He approached the woman and looked at her black dress, which perfectly matched the tone of her lipstick and hair.

"You look beautiful."

"You're not bad either." Cordelia laughed and kissed the judge's cheeks.

The man reached out and guided the woman to the car. He opened the door and allowed her entry. Cordelia closed the door and waited for her date to enter the vehicle. When

Edgar sat down and put on his seat belt, she asked, "Where are we going?"

"Why do you ask?"

"Because you told me to dress up. It's not that often that someone takes me to a fancy place."

"The perks of dating a judge," Edgar said.

"I am not dating you," Cordelia replied.

"Yet," the man said and laughed as he drove down her driveway.

Cordelia smiled and turned her head to admire the city. The moon shone in the starry sky, making the evening even more beautiful. Minutes later they finally arrived at the restaurant. Cordelia gasped when she realized Edgar had taken her to dinner at Mon Petit, the fanciest and most expensive French restaurant in town.

The parking valet opened the door and helped Cordelia step out of the car. Edgar met her on the other side and took her arm. They walked inside together and asked for a table.

Once they sat down, the waiter approached. The judge ordered a bottle of the house's best wine, two glasses, and a plate of escargot as an appetizer. As they began to talk, Cordelia was amazed by the vast knowledge Edgar Dunning had on every subject. It was like he had studied just so he could talk to her.

The wine and escargot arrived. As the waiter walked away, he said he'd be back later to take their orders. As they ate, Cordelia and her companion continued talking, and Edgar continued to surprise her. The judge was not only a highly educated man but he was also handsome, charming, and elegant. The only thing that Cordelia hated was the fact that even though he had so many qualities, the judge could be very pompous, which bothered her.

Once they finished their appetizers, the waiter returned and asked if they were ready to place their order. The judge ordered his plate, and before Cordelia could say what she wanted, he ordered for her. The lad looked at Cordelia, and she smiled, embarrassed.

"Don't worry. You will love this dish," Edgar said.

"I'm sure I will," she replied.

After they finished the food, the judged ordered the dessert he wanted to share with Cordelia. The waiter returned a couple of minutes later with a plate containing two scoops of vanilla ice cream and a small chocolate cake with hot fudge inside. The couple finished dessert in less than ten minutes and asked for the check. When the waiter returned with the check, he waited beside the table for the judge to analyze the items. While Dunning looked at the check, the waiter turned to Cordelia and asked, "Did you enjoy your meal, Mrs. Cordelia?"

"I sure did, James."

"That's good to hear. I was a bit surprised when you didn't order the usual."

"The usual?" Edgar Dunning asked, staring at the waiter and Cordelia, completely stunned.

"Oh yeah," James said. "Mrs. Cordelia has come here for years now. They all speak very highly of her. She's one of our best customers."

"Really?"

"Yes, Edgar," Cordelia replied. "I don't think you know this, but I do know how to behave in a fancy place. And I can pick my own expensive food."

Cordelia stood up and opened her purse. She gave two ten-dollar bills to the waiter, and he thanked her.

"You deserve it, James. Your service was great, as always."

"Thank you, milady," James said with a brief bow.

Cordelia turned to face Edgar and said, "As for you, don't ever come after me again."

She smiled and walked away. Edgar Dunning looked at James, who smirked before he left. The judge sat there for a moment, completely flabbergasted but also amazed. After he thought for a moment, he came to the conclusion that Cordelia Mackenzie could be just as pompous as he was.

~oOo~

After lunchtime Carla heard the doorbell ring. She opened the door and encountered a woman she had never seen before—at least that was what she thought.

"Hello, I am Susan Abromheit. I'd like to speak to Matt."

"You're Clark's sister," Carla said in shock.

"I suppose you're Matt's mother. Yes, I am his sister," Susan answered. "It's a pleasure to meet you."

"The pleasure is all mine. Would you like to come inside?"

Susan smiled and entered. Carla closed the door and took her visitor to the living room. Susan sat on the couch, and then Carla called Matt, who was in his bedroom. He came downstairs, and his mother followed a couple of minutes later. Susan stood up and hugged the boy. Once they parted, they sat on the couch, and Carla took the chair next to the window.

"I was hoping you'd show up."

"Oh yeah," Susan said and laughed. "I was trying to find your address. I had to visit Adriana in jail to find out."

"How is she?" Carla asked.

"A bit different from what we're used to, but she's good," Susan explained. "Being confined somewhere is extremely difficult. I speak from experience."

Carla gulped and stood up. She went to the kitchen and returned a few minute later carrying a tray with three glasses and a pitcher of lemonade. Matt helped his mother serve the refreshments and then returned to his seat.

"Well," Susan said as she drank her lemonade. "The reason for my visit is very simple. I came to thank you, Matt. The day you walked into my room and told me your story, you gave me hope. Hope that I had lost years ago!"

"You don't have to thank me."

"The love you have for your mother is something impressive. You put your life at risk to uncover the truth and save her from something extremely bad. So here's what I have to offer."

Susan put her glass on the coffee table and opened her purse. She pulled out a check and handed it to Matt. His eyes widened as he saw the value. He showed the check to his mother, who stifled a scream.

"Susan, this is more than generous, but we can't take that."

"Yes you can, and you will!" Susan said firmly. "You rescued me from my fifteen-year confinement, I couldn't do anything else."

"But do you have this kind of money to give?" Carla asked, standing up. "I understand that Clark lost everything."

"Not my money," Susan explained. "When I worked in advertising, I was one of the best. I saved a lot of money, and Clark had no idea. So please accept this check. I know it seems wrong, but I have to do something for you."

"Well, we thank you," Matt said, embracing his friend. "Really."

Matt, Carla, and Susan talked for a few more hours until Susan decided it was time to go. Carla and her son accompanied the visitor to the door. She said good-bye and walked down the porch steps. When she was halfway between the house and the sidewalk, Matt called to her.

"Yes?"

"Will you go back home?"

"For now," Susan answered, "but I'll sell it. Too many bad memories there."

"That's good," Carla commented. "See you around."

"We sure will. I'll send some news. Hope you do that too."

"We will!" Matt said.

Susan smiled and walked away. As Susan drove off, Carla looked across the street and saw her family gathered at Carlota's front yard. They were observing the moving truck that had just arrived on the street. Carlota waved at them to come over. When they got there, Matt asked, "What do we know?"

"Not much," Mery answered. "But they seem rich. Look at the furniture."

"The furniture tells me they have really bad taste," Carlota replied.

"And since when do rich people have good taste?" Ana asked.

A few minutes later a minivan approached the house. The vehicle stopped at the driveway, and the driver cut the engine. While the movers carried the furniture inside the house, the family stepped out of their car.

The first person who jumped of the vehicle was a woman. She was tall, slender, and extremely beautiful. Her black hair and pouty lips drew the attention of anyone who looked at her. The husband, a strong, gray-haired man, was extremely handsome. And finally the couple's son emerged. He was a couple of months younger than Matt. He was thin and strong, and he looked very much like his father, except for his eyes, which belonged to his mother.

"Wow," Thales said. "She's beautiful."

"She certainly is," Carla commented. "Look at her hair. What the hell am I doing wrong?"

The new family looked around and saw the Mackenzie family. The woman smiled, which made her look even more beautiful, and then waved to the neighbors. The Mackenzies returned the gesture. The new family crossed the street and approached the Mackenzies.

"Hello, I'm Elizabeth Phillips. This is my husband, Jackson, and our son, Michael."

"Hi," Jackson said.

"How's it going?" Michael asked.

"Oh, hello!" Carlota said. "I'm Carlota Mackenzie. These are my daughters, Cordelia, Mery, and Ana. Carla and Thales are my grandchildren. And this is Matt, my great-grandson."

The Mackenzie family greeted the new neighbors, who seemed quite friendly. Elizabeth opened her purse and pulled her sunglasses out of a black box. She put the box away and put on her glasses.

"Very sunny today."

"Oh, tell me about it," Ana said. "I've used gallons of sunscreen already."

"So," Matt said, "where do you come from?"

"Los Angeles," Michael answered.

"Ah," Cordelia said. "Big city."

"I'm sorry for the intrusion," Carlota commented, "but what made you leave a city like LA for a small town like Greendale?"

"It was too much," Elizabeth answered. "LA is a wonderful city, but we couldn't handle the confusions over the day-to-day, so we decided to move."

"Well, I think we should be going," Jackson said. "We've got much to do."

"You're right," Elizabeth agreed. "We'll see you another time. Maybe at the barbecue we're having this weekend."

"Sounds great," Mery answered. "See you later."

"Bye," Michael said, waving at his neighbors.

The Phillips walked away and entered their new home. The Mackenzies stood on Carlota's lawn for a few more minutes until she said, "Well, I've gotta get going. I have a doctor's appointment."

"What for?" Ana asked.

"Nothing. Just a checkup."

Carlota said good-bye to their relatives and entered her car. She drove off and left the street. The remaining members of the family stayed there for a few more hours until they decided to go back to their homes.

CHAPTER
15

Thanksgiving

THERE WAS ONLY ONE WEEK left before Thanksgiving. The residents of Crystal Street started to decorate their homes with some ornaments. The dinner guest lists started to be made, as well as party announcements.

But the fact that caught people's attention the most was the fact that Diane Thompson, the former mayor's widow, had booked a room for a luncheon she'd throw for her most intimate friends. And everyone was eager to know if their names were going to make the list.

During the week, Diane distributed the invitations for her party. And as expected, she invited all the members of the Mackenzie family, including Robert. She distributed the rest of her invitations on Friday, and the luncheon was scheduled to take place on Thursday of the next week.

All those invited to Diane's party were eager for the day to arrive. Even those who were not called were excited, as they were dying to see the news about the party.

~oOo~

The days passed in a flash. When the members of the Mackenzie family looked at their calendars, there were only two days left before the luncheon. On Tuesday Robert decided to visit his son and his ex-wife to give them some news.

He arrived at their home, and he saw Matt sitting on the bench, reading a book. The boy greeted his father, and Robert asked him to call his mother so they could talk. Matt entered his house and called his mother. They returned a few minutes later and found Robert sitting on the stairs. Carla stared at the man and crossed her arms. Robert stood up and smiled.

"What do you want?" Carla asked. "I'm busy."

"The three of us need to talk," Robert said. "I have something to tell you."

"Is it something serious?" Matt asked, putting his book under his arm.

"I'm moving."

At that moment, Matt let his book fall to the ground, and Carla gasped. The boy stepped back and sat on the porch's swing. Robert's expression, however, remained neutral. Carla approached her ex-husband and said firmly, "How dare you? You come back after years and say that you wanna have a relationship with your son, but now you're leaving?"

"I was trying, and I was almost being able to forgive you," Matt said, standing up. "But now I see you will never change. You'll always be the same Robert."

"What?" Robert exclaimed. "No, I just bought Helena's old house! I'm moving to Crystal Street!"

Carla's eyes widened as much as Matt's. Robert laughed and hugged them at the same time. Matt took a deep breath and asked, "Are you sure you're not going away?"

"No!" Robert celebrated. "Isn't that great? I'm closer, and we can spend more time together."

"Oh God," Carla said. "This is going to be hell."

~oOo~

Cordelia was in the kitchen, slicing a carrot to throw into the stew. She had invited her daughter and grandson to eat with her that day. When she finished cutting the carrot, Cordelia lit the fire on the stove and put the pot of water over the flame.

She got all the vegetable slices and threw everything in the container. Then she took a potato to the sink so she could start peeling it, but then the doorbell rang. Cordelia rolled her eyes and threw the tubercle on the counter and left the kitchen.

When Cordelia opened the door, her first impulse was to close it, but Edgar Dunning stopped her and walked in the house. She stepped back while she pointed her finger at the man. He kept coming closer.

"Get out of my house!" she said with anger. "I told you I didn't wanna see you anymore."

"But we need to talk," the judge said.

"I have nothing to say to you. Go away, or I'll call the police."

"I'm a judge," Edgar said and laughed.

"Judge or not, this is an invasion of privacy! I want you out of here!" Cordelia yelled.

Edgar stopped moving, and so did Cordelia. They were silent for several minutes until the man said, "I feel … I behaved terribly wrong at the restaurant. I treated you in an abominable way."

"No," Cordelia replied, "you were beyond abominable because you already are an abominable, disgusting, despicable, ugly, and pompous person!"

"And you're gonna tell me you're not pompous?" Dunning said and laughed. "We're alike! You were extremely pompous when you left the restaurant."

"I was not!" Cordelia yelled, outraged.

"Of course you were. And I must say I was fascinated."

"You're sick!"

Edgar gave a hussy laugh and ran toward the woman. Cordelia let out a scream, but it was too late to flee because the judge already had her in his arms. She started to struggle and slap the man, trying to get away from him, but Edgar had a firm grip.

"Let go of me."

"Have you ever heard that phrase, 'Opposites attract?' That's the biggest lie. We have so much in common. That's because we were meant to be together."

"No! Absolutely not! Let me go, you freak!"

"I want you, Cordelia, and you want me," Dunning said.

"I don't want you! You're despicable!"

"Oh yeah?"

The judge did not hesitate. He held Cordelia's head and gave her a kiss. She did not resist at first, but soon she pushed herself away and wiped her lips. Edgar was smiling, and she was disgusted.

"Oh my God," Cordelia said as she approached the man. "I hate you!"

"No, you don't."

Edgar grabbed the woman by the arm and pulled her to him and gave her another kiss. When he released her, Cordelia said, "Disgusting!"

When Edgar approached her, things changed. Cordelia grabbed the judge, pushed him against the wall, and kissed him. He looked at her smiling and asked, "What do you think of me now?"

"I still hate you, you disgusting, despicable man!"

Edgar burst out laughing, while Cordelia hugged and kissed him again. The man wrapped his arms around her and carried her. She let out a scandalous laugh and said, "You are crazy!"

"Is your bedroom upstairs?"

"No," Cordelia said, unbuttoning her blouse, "let's use the sofa!"

~oOo~

Diane Thompson arrived at Carlota's house just before noon. She rang the bell, but nobody answered. The widow rang the bell three more times, but she still didn't get any answer. Diane raised an eyebrow and walked to the garage. She saw Carlota's car and scratched her head.

"What is going on?" Diane asked herself.

She returned to the front door and turned the knob. The door slid open, and the woman entered. The lower floor was deserted. Diane called for her friend, but Carlota didn't say a thing. The widow walked through the living room and decided to go upstairs.

Once she was on the second floor, Diane went to Carlota's room. That was locked. The woman knocked on the door, and just like before, she didn't get an answer. She knocked a few more times and called for her friend.

"Carlota, please open up. I know you're in there."

"Go away!" Carlota shouted from the inside. "I want to be alone!"

"Honey, please open the door. I'm worried," Diane said. "We were going to lunch today, remember?"

"I said go away!"

"Carlota! Open this door! Open it right now!"

Diane heard the door being unlocked. The doorknob turned, and Carlota appeared. The widow sighed at the sight of her friend. Carlota's eye makeup was smeared, and her eyes were puffy and red from crying.

"Oh my God, Carlota, what happened?"

"I don't wanna talk about it," Carlota replied before she blew her noise into a tissue.

"Honey," Diane commented, "you can talk to me. What happened?"

Carlota rolled her eyes and allowed her friend to enter. They sat on the bed and were silent for a few minutes. Carlota wiped her tears, cleared her throat, and said, "I went to the doctor yesterday."

"Why?"

"Just a normal checkup. I was feeling nausea, some pain. So I decided to run some tests and see if everything was okay," Carlota explained. "The results came back today."

"Oh, is it something serious?"

"It seems that I have lung cancer."

"Carlota, my God," Diane said, touching her chest. "Have you told anyone?"

"No," Carlota replied, "I've only told you."

"But what about your family?"

"They don't need to know yet. I'll tell them, but not just yet."

"Carlota," Diane protested.

"Diane, don't make me regret telling you," Carlota said. "Promise me you won't say a thing at the luncheon."

"Fine, I promise. But you'll have to tell them eventually!"

~oOo~

While Carla and her son walked to Cordelia's house, they talked about the recent news Robert had just given them earlier that day. While Matt seemed to face the situation in a positive way, Carla couldn't stop complaining.

"I know it's hard—"

"No, you don't," she said. "I hate him, Matt."

"I know you do. You've already told me this countless times," the boy commented. "I know that what he did was wrong. But now he's back, and he's really trying to be the father he never was. You should be happy, and you know what? I also hated him for most of my life."

"Do you love him?"

"I do not," Matt confirmed. "I'm still getting used to this whole situation."

Carla rolled her eyes and pulled her hair back in a long ponytail. They continued walking until she asked, "Do you think he's changed?"

"I didn't know him before," Matt said. "But he's a good person. And you should be grateful because he's the one who helped me to talk to Susan."

"I know," Carla snapped. "And this is what pisses me off. I didn't wanna owe the man who walked out on me."

"You don't owe him anything. But you should try to be nicer."

Carla nodded and slapped her son's head. The boy let out an *ouch* and laughed. Carla laughed too, and then he asked, "What was that for?"

"For telling me I'm not nice."

They continued laughing until they got to Cordelia's house. Carla rang the doorbell, but no one appeared. She rang the bell a few more times until Cordelia finally arrived at the door. She was all disheveled, and her blouse was barely buttoned. Her makeup, especially her lipstick, was smeared. Carla and Matt stared at the woman, completely surprised by her state of disarray.

"Mother?" Carla asked. "Are you okay?"

"Yes," Cordelia said, out of breath.

"Good, because I'm hungry!" Matt said.

"Umm … lunch is not ready. I had an unforeseen—"

"What happened?" Matt asked, raising an eyebrow.

"Well—"

"Honey! Where are my pants?" Edgar yelled from inside the house.

Cordelia closed her eyes, embarrassed. Matt and Carla looked at each other and then stared at her. Cordelia gave a slight smile, and her daughter and grandson burst out laughing. Cordelia took a deep breath and said, "I'm sorry."

"Don't be," Carla said. "I'm glad to see that you're having fun."

"Yeah." Matt nodded, trying to hold back his laughter. "Mom and I can have lunch somewhere else."

"Sushi?" Carla asked.

"Sushi!" the boy replied.

They said good-bye to Cordelia and walked away, laughing. The woman slapped her forehead and went back inside the house.

~oOo~

The day finally arrived for the luncheon. The ballroom Diane reserved for the event was beautifully decorated. The tables were arranged in a way so that the dance floor was free for those who'd like to enjoy the sound of the band that would play after dessert.

It was shortly after noon when the guests started to arrive. Diane welcomed everyone personally and settled everyone in their seats. The members of the Mackenzie family were the last ones to arrive, but Diane greeted them with even greater enthusiasm.

As her guests of honor, Diane had placed them at her own table. They organized themselves, and the party started. Matt sat next to his aunt Mery, but he left an empty seat between him and Carla for when Sarah arrived. Robert sat next to Carla, who did not like this decision one bit.

"C'mon, Carla. Crack a smile!"

"Don't talk to me, Robert!" Carla said sternly. "I am very angry!"

"What's wrong with your mother and Robert?" Mery whispered in her nephew's ear.

"Ah … he's moving to Crystal Street," Matt answered. "Mom is not happy."

"Damn!" Mery commented. "This will be hell!"

Matt laughed and continued his conversation with his aunt. Across the table Carlota, Ana, and Diane were indulging in an engaging conversation about the situation of the new mayor. Oddly enough, the widow believed that the current one was doing a much better job than her late husband had done.

"And I don't say this because I was cheated on. David was a great man, but what the mayor is doing is absolutely fantastic!"

"I agree with you, Diane," Ana said. "Kelly is doing an excellent job, especially with public transportation."

"Indeed," Carlota commented. "I dare say that in the near future Greendale may cease to be a mere suburb."

"Probably," Diane said. "If Kelly gets reelected, I am sure Greendale will grow considerably."

After a few more minutes, Diane stood up and walked to the center of the room. One of the waiters brought her a microphone so that everyone could hear what she had to say. The widow cleared her throat and smiled.

"Welcome! It is more than a pleasure to have all of you here today. I know that many of you found it weird for me to throw a party so soon after my husband's recent passing. But I believe that life goes on. Losing David was the hardest thing for me, but I am sure he wouldn't like to see me in a state of eternal depression, so I decided to throw this party because I believe that even in the hardest moments we always have something to be thankful for. And isn't that what we do on Thanksgiving? I'm thankful for the best forty years beside my husband. Although certain things did not go as I had planned, David was and still is the love of my life."

Diane raised her champagne glass and said, "I propose a toast! To all those things we are thankful for! Let us give thanks! May God bless you all!"

The room filled with the sound of glasses clicking while people toasted. When they all lowered their glasses, they all applauded Diane, and she shed a few tears. She wiped her cheeks and said, "Lunch is served! Thank you all for coming."

Diane returned to her seat while the guests went to the buffet line. Members of the Mackenzie family remained in their seats, waiting for the line to shrink so that they could get their food. As they talked, Matt spotted Sarah, who had just arrived. He stood and ran toward his girlfriend. He kissed her, but she stepped away.

"Is everything okay?"

"No," Sarah replied, rubbing her forehead.

"What happened? Are you mad at me?" Matt asked, worried.

"No, it's not you. It's us."

"You wanna break up?"

"No!" Sarah exclaimed. "I just don't know how to tell you this."

"Babe, you're scaring me. What happened?"

"I'm pregnant."

"What?" Matt exclaimed in shock. "When? How? Where?"

"I don't know. I'm a month pregnant."

"Hello, Sarah," Carla said, approaching. "I thought you weren't coming."

Matt smiled idiotically at his mother, and Sarah stammered for a bit but still managed to answer her. "No, I came. I just had some issues to solve before coming."

"Well, I'm glad you could make it. Now, you two, go get some food."

Carla smiled and walked away. Matt waited a few seconds before he turned to his girlfriend. "Have you told anyone about this?"

"No, I've only told you and my doctor. My mom thinks I went to the dentist."

"Okay. We can't tell anyone else. We have to think."

"I agree."

Hours passed by, and then the band finally took the stage. The members of the group introduced themselves and started to play. Some guests moved to the dance floor while others danced next to their tables.

"Diane, this is without doubt your best party."

"Thank you, Cordelia."

While everyone enjoyed themselves, Thales fiddled with his cell phone. He seemed too distracted by what he was doing. A few minutes later, Ana approached her son and asked, "What are you doing? Shouldn't you be dancing?"

"I'm talking to Michael," Thales replied.

"Michael? Michael Phillips, the new neighbor?"

"Yes."

"I didn't know you two were friends."

"A bit, yeah," Thales said. "And answering your other question, I don't like this band."

"Okay. Stay there. But if you wanna go home, take the car. I can get a ride with one of the girls."

"No, I'm staying."

The boy smiled and returned to his conversation. Ana walked away and met with her sisters on the dance floor. To relieve their tension, Matt and Sarah decided to dance as well, while Robert still attempted to cheer up his ex-wife. In another corner, Diane and Carlota talked about the recent illness Carlota had discovered.

"So what did the doctor say?" Diane asked.

"He said I should start chemo within two weeks."

"That's good, but what about the cancer? Is it only in your lungs?"

"Dr. Blake told me that for now it's only in my lungs, yes. I was lucky to find out early on, so we'll just keep an eye—"

"I'm sure everything will be all right, honey," Diane said, running her hand over her friend's shoulder. "You have strength, determination, and fiber. You'll do it wonderfully well."

"Thank you."

Diane smiled and walked away. Carlota looked at her family members and smiled as well. It was in that moment that she realized the right thing to do. After the party she'd tell her relatives about her recent situation and how she'd face it head-on.

While Carlota dealt with her thoughts, Carla was finally able to show Robert a smile, and the two decided to join the others on the dance floor. Moments later Edgar Dunning arrived at the luncheon and met Cordelia and asked her to dance.

It was a great party. Everyone was happy, and they all had fun. And they would remember that day for a long while.

~oOo~

Elizabeth Phillips locked a small wooden box and put it under her bed later that night. Her husband, Jackson, came out of the bathroom and lay down beside her. They were quiet for a while until he said, "Are you all right?"

"I'm fine," she replied before she kissed her husband. "I think this can be a great new start for us."

"I was thinking the same thing."

"But aren't you scared?"

"Why would I be?" Jackson asked. "I think you are being silly. We have nothing else to worry about."

"Yeah, I guess you are right. I am being silly," Elizabeth said and smiled. "We just need to be careful—that's all."

"Exactly. Besides, we are nice people. No one is going to suspect us."

Elizabeth smiled and kissed her husband one last time before she turned off the light.

About the Author

Matheus Beltrão Oliveira e Silva was born in Brazil. He is now a student of journalism at Indiana University-Purdue University in Indianapolis, Indiana. He is the author of *The Cosmic Stone*.

Printed in the United States
By Bookmasters